QUESTION OF GUILT

SALLY RIGBY

Storm
PUBLISHING

This is a work of fiction. Names, characters, businesses, places, events and incidents are either the products of the author's imagination or used in a fictitious manner. Any resemblance to actual persons, living or dead, or actual events is purely coincidental.

Copyright © Sally Rigby, 2025

The moral right of the author has been asserted.

All rights reserved. No part of this book may be reproduced or used in any manner without the prior written permission of the copyright owner. This prohibition includes, but is not limited to, any reproduction or use for the purpose of training artificial intelligence technologies or systems.

To request permissions, contact the publisher at rights@stormpublishing.co

Ebook ISBN: 978-1-80508-629-1
Paperback ISBN: 978-1-80508-630-7

Cover design: Stuart Bache
Cover images: Shutterstock

Published by Storm Publishing.
For further information, visit:
www.stormpublishing.co

ALSO BY SALLY RIGBY

Cavendish & Walker Series

Deadly Games

Fatal Justice

Death Track

Lethal Secret

Last Breath

Final Verdict

Ritual Demise

Mortal Remains

Silent Graves

Kill Shot

Dark Secrets

Broken Screams

Death's Shadow

A Cornwall Murder Mystery

The Lost Girls of Penzance

The Hidden Graves of St Ives

Murder at Land's End

The Camborne Killings

Death at Porthcurno Cove

Detective Sebastian Clifford Series

Web of Lies

Speak No Evil
Never Too Late
Hidden From Sight
Fear the Truth
Wake the Past

PROLOGUE

She knew they'd come eventually. She'd rehearsed it in her mind a hundred times, though she hadn't expected him to show up at her front door. She thought it would be at one of the meetings, or somewhere away from her home.

The sight of the well-dressed man standing there, immaculate in his tailored suit, sent a flutter of recognition through her chest – not fear, but vindication. She was clearly getting close enough to rattle them. They must have been watching... waiting for her husband to leave for work.

The other man, stockier and less smartly attired, shifted uncomfortably beside his employer. A hired hand, clearly, probably meant to do the dirty work. She smiled, stepping back from her doorway with practised casualness, inviting them in. Let them think they had the upper hand. Let them believe she was naive enough to hope for answers.

Her daughter's school photos lined the hallway, marking the years like rings in a tree. Seven, ten, thirteen. The hired man's eyes lingered on them as they passed. Good. Let him see her humanity. Let him understand what he was party to.

They settled in her kitchen at the table, apart from the hired man, who leant against the door frame like he wanted to bolt, while his employer sat with the easy confidence of someone who'd never faced consequences.

'You need to back off,' the well-dressed man said, his voice smooth as chocolate. 'Consider this a friendly warning.'

Her resolve didn't waver. She'd spent months gathering evidence, building her case piece by piece. She was the grain of sand in their perfectly oiled machine, and she intended to grind their gears to a halt. 'Or what?' she asked, though she already knew. Men like him didn't make house calls for friendly warnings.

The hired man's discomfort grew palpable as his employer's request for cooperation turned to threats, then to orders. When commanded to 'get heavy', she saw the man's resolve crack. He looked at her daughter's photos on the windowsill, then shook his head.

'Listen,' he pled. 'If you love your family—'

'That's exactly why I'm doing this,' she cut him off. 'Because I love my family. Because I love other people's families. Because someone must stop men like him from thinking they're untouchable.'

The well-dressed man's patience snapped and his veneer of civilisation dropped from his face like a discarded mask. As he approached with the rope, she kept her eyes fixed on him, refusing to look away. She wouldn't give him the satisfaction of her fear, even as the hired man's trembling hands secured her arms.

When the well-dressed man reached into his coat pocket, she knew with sudden clarity that she had miscalculated. She'd imagined violence, yes, but not this – not the small capsule he held between manicured fingers. Not the cold efficiency with which he approached her. Her last thought, as he forced the cyanide past her lips, and washed it down with some cold coffee from the mug that had been on the table, was not of failure or fear, but of hope. Hope that her death would accomplish what her life had not: exposing the truth about men who thought their money made them gods.

She was wrong about that, too.

ONE

Monday, 14 July

'On a scale of one to ten, how important do you think it is to have a roof?'

Sebastian Clifford, who had been working on a final report for a client, glanced over to where Lucinda 'Birdie' Bird was sitting on the reading chair in the corner of their office. After four years of being partners, he could usually tell when she was joking, but there were still moments when he wasn't sure.

'Uh... Depends on whether you like water or not.'

Birdie let out a dramatic sigh and put down her phone. 'Why is it so hard to find the perfect place to buy? This "hidden gem" isn't even the worst one I've looked at. There was a charming "doer-upper" which was mouldy from top to bottom with a gaping hole in the lounge ceiling. And don't tell me the right one will come along, or I'll scream.'

'I'll definitely pass on that,' he said. 'Having heard you on the cricket pitch, I don't think my ears could cope in such an enclosed space.'

When they'd first met, and Birdie was a detective constable

with Market Harborough police force, she'd been saving to buy her own house, but after joining him at Clifford Investigation Services, she'd invested her savings to make her an equal partner. Now they were well established, she'd decided to take the plunge and start looking for a property again.

'Listen to you cracking a joke so early in the morning.' Birdie stood up and stretched. Elsa, Seb's yellow Labrador, who'd been lying at the foot of the reading chair, raised one large, brown eye, no doubt wondering whether she was going to have a second breakfast or a walk. Birdie paused to pat the dog, then returned to her desk. 'I should make you view some properties with me as a reminder we don't all live in seventeenth-century mansions.'

'Which I don't own, remember? I might need to look for a roofless "hidden gem" of my own soon. Sarah isn't going to stay away forever.'

Seb had an apartment in London, but after visiting East Farndon for his cousin Sarah's husband's funeral, he'd stayed on at Rendall Hall at her request to look into his death. It was during the investigation that he'd first met Birdie. After the case had been solved, Sarah had gone travelling and had asked Seb to become a long-term house minder for her home. She'd talked about returning to the UK last year, but since then she'd put back her plans to return because of meeting someone. But that didn't mean she'd be staying away forever.

'Good luck finding somewhere to suit you, your equally tall daughter, and your garden-loving dog. Which reminds me, when's Keira due back?' Birdie asked, referring to Seb's nineteen-year-old daughter, who'd been visiting her grandparents in London after finishing university for the summer.

'Sometime tomorrow.'

Seb had only known about his daughter for eighteen months but they already shared a special bond, made even closer by him being her only parent following the death of her mother.

'I bet you can't wait,' Birdie replied as the doorbell rang. 'That'll be our ten o'clock appointment. Daryl Brackstone. She refused to say what she wanted to discuss when I spoke to her yesterday, but she sounded nervous. I'll bring her through in case she's disturbed by your stature.'

'I'll think small thoughts,' he promised, and Birdie groaned before disappearing into the hallway. Though she had a point. It wasn't unusual for their clients to be anxious, and while being six foot six was useful at times, it could also be intimidating.

He abandoned his desk for the reading chair that Birdie had so recently deserted and sat down. There was a sofa across from it and a coffee table in the middle. Elsa made a snuffling noise, and he tickled her nose as Birdie returned to the room, followed by their new client.

Daryl Brackstone appeared to be in her fifties. She had short brown hair and was wearing a floral blouse with a pair of wide-legged trousers. Her eyes were wide, and her gaze darted around the room, like she'd been called in to see the headmaster for doing something wrong. But then she straightened her shoulders, as if convincing herself to go through with the appointment.

'Daryl, this is Sebastian Clifford,' Birdie said, making the introduction.

'Nice to meet you.' He extended a hand, only half standing. 'I hope you didn't encounter any problems finding us.'

'Not at all. Thank you for seeing me at such short notice. I'm still in two minds about whether this is a good idea.' Daryl settled on one end of the sofa and put her large leather bag onto her lap, clutching it as if it were a life raft.

'We understand,' Birdie assured her. 'Which is why we like to have an initial consultation before going ahead with any investigation. Rest assured that whatever you tell us will be treated with the utmost confidence.'

'I appreciate that, thank you.' Daryl's fingers fiddled with the bag straps for several seconds. Neither Seb nor Birdie made any effort to speak. Most of their clients only came to see them when there was something wrong in their lives, and it was often difficult for them to talk about it. 'I'm not sure where to begin,' she eventually said. 'Are either of you from around here?'

'I'm from Market Harborough, but Seb's from down south,' Birdie explained.

Again, there was silence as Daryl's fingers continued to weave in and out of the straps. Finally, she looked up at them both.

'Birdie, you might be too young to remember, but in 1989, a woman was murdered. My mother, Helen. She was killed in our family home in Market Harborough. She was only thirty-seven when it happened. My father, Wes, was charged almost immediately and found guilty. He was given a life sentence. He died a year ago in prison.' It was clear from the weary tone that she'd told the story too many times.

'That must have been very difficult for you. I assume you were at school when she died?' Seb said.

Since moving into the area, he'd come across several shocking cases from the past, but not the murder of a housewife by her husband.

'That's right. I was fourteen.' Daryl's knuckles had turned white as her hands clenched her bag. 'It was awful. Even now, I feel like I've had two lives: one that stopped the day she was killed, and one that started the day after.'

'I can only imagine how hard that must have been.' Birdie's expression was solemn. 'Do you believe your father was guilty?'

Colour flooded the woman's cheeks and her shoulders stiffened. 'No. Never. He wasn't like that. But no one asked me what I thought, and I was too distraught to comprehend what was happening. By the time I came out of the initial fog and grief, it was like I'd lost both my parents... one to death and the other to prison. That's why I'm here. I'd like to clear his name, even if it is posthumously. I need to find out the truth about what happened.' She dropped her head and dabbed at her eyes with a tissue that had been scrunched up in her hand.

Seb waited until she was composed before gently probing. 'If your father died in prison, why wait until now to consider hiring someone to look into it?'

'There are a couple of reasons. For a long time, I had no idea where to start, and then life got busy with my job and raising my daughter. But recently I was contacted by Ali Simmons. She has her own podcast and lives in Leicester. Have you heard of her?'

At the mention of the word *podcast*, Seb and Birdie exchanged a look.

There had been a huge increase in true-crime podcasts and amateur detectives on the internet in recent years, and while some of them seemed methodical in their research and rigorous in their conclusions, others appeared to be more interested in wild theories and conspiracies. Or, in extreme cases, glorifying the murderers at the expense of the surviving families and friends of the victims, who ended up being retraumatised.

'I recall seeing the name but haven't listened to any of her shows,' Seb answered, speaking first.

'I haven't heard of her,' Birdie added. 'You said she contacted you, so does that mean she's been looking into the case?'

Daryl nodded. 'Yes, and I know what you're thinking. I was sceptical at first. I can't begin to tell you how painful it is whenever the case gets dragged up in the press or is discussed in online forums or podcasts. But Ali's different. She'd done a lot of research and wanted to be upfront with me about it. She believes there were issues with the original investigation.'

'I see,' Seb said. 'What has she discovered that might prove your father was wrongly convicted?'

'My mother was poisoned by potassium cyanide in her coffee. The police found pesticide in the garage, which contained cyanide, and concluded that my father used it to poison her. But Ali said that the evidence is weak and circumstantial.'

Seb rubbed his chin, agreeing that the police's version of the facts could be problematic.

'She would've tasted it,' Birdie said, voicing Seb's own thoughts.

'Exactly. Ali's investigated the level of cyanide that would have been needed to kill my mum, and it's unlikely she would have drunk enough of the coffee, considering the taste of the pesticide.'

'Does Ali have a theory regarding how the poison got into your mum's drink then?' Birdie asked, leaning forward, her interest obviously piqued.

'With a potassium cyanide capsule. I believe that means the taste and smell would be more easily disguised. Or it could have been forced into her mouth with coffee following to wash it down.'

So far the reasoning had been purely speculative, and without knowing which forensic tests were carried out at the time, or having access to the samples, Seb believed it would be virtually impossible to investigate the podcaster's theory without any other evidence. He kept his voice neutral as he asked, 'What else did Ms Simmons discover?'

'A neighbour from across the road testified at the trial that my father's car was in the driveway when my mother was murdered. Because this meant the police could place him at the scene, they concluded that he'd done it. The thing is, her view of our driveway was obstructed by a huge tree that would have blocked her window, so I don't know how she could have seen his car. The tree was removed many years ago, but I still have photos of it. It wasn't until Ali mentioned it that I remembered about the tree. Also, this neighbour made two contradictory statements at the time regarding my father's car being there.'

'Did the podcaster come up with anything else?' Seb asked.

'Yes, she said that the police didn't bother to investigate other avenues. They decided my father was guilty and pursued that instead of digging deeper.' Daryl looked up, her eyes imploring. 'So, what do you think? Is this the sort of case you'd be interested in taking?'

'We'd like to speak to Ali Simmons and do our own research before making a final decision. We need to ensure there's enough substance to move forward,' Birdie said in a kind but firm voice.

'Cold cases can be difficult,' Seb added. 'Especially one from thirty-six years ago. Gaining access to information is likely to be challenging. Most of it won't have been digitised. Plus, witnesses and officers working the case may well have moved away, or are no longer alive. There's also the cost of hiring us for you to consider, especially when the outcome might not be what you're hoping.'

For the first time, there was a confidence enveloping Daryl Brackstone and she returned his gaze.

'I have money put aside, and if this can give me and my daughter some peace, I would consider it well spent. I don't want my grandchildren to grow up in the shadow of this case. It might also give me back some of my childhood memories. If there was a miscarriage of justice... I *need* to know about it.'

'I understand. As Birdie said, we'll do some preliminary research and visit Ali Simmons, after which we'll be in touch.'

'Thank you. I'll give you her details. She hasn't yet posted the podcast about my mother's murder, but she said she'd be happy to discuss it with you.' Daryl got to her feet. 'Now I'd better be on my way.'

They walked with Daryl to her car and were soon joined by Elsa, who wandered over to the far side of the garden. The July sun was accompanied by a gentle breeze, which caused the delphiniums and lupins to sway. The idyllic scene was always such a contrast to the kind of work they did. But that suited Seb, because it helped him not to focus solely on the darker side of human nature.

'Well?' Birdie asked as they strolled across the newly mown grass after their potential new client had disappeared down the gravel driveway. 'Has this podcaster given Daryl false hope?'

'Quite possibly. Are you familiar with the case?'

Birdie nodded. 'I wasn't born then, but it was sometimes mentioned at the station. I do know the house on Northampton Road where it happened. It's quite fancy, but kids would avoid it at Halloween because they said it was haunted by the victim.' She pulled out her phone then hesitated. 'The timing's niggling me. Why is the podcaster digging now, after all these years?'

The breeze stirred the flowers again, and Seb watched a bee drift between the lupins. In his experience, cold cases rarely remained cold without input. Someone was always working to keep them that way.

'Call Ali Simmons and arrange a visit. We need to know what questions she's been asking, and who might be getting nervous about the answers.'

TWO

Tuesday, 15 July

Ali Simmons lived in the centre of Leicester in a historic Grade II-listed red-brick warehouse. The four-storey building had been sympathetically restored and was flanked by a small lawn.

Seb parked up outside, and Birdie whistled as they passed several top-of-the-range cars on their way to the front entrance.

'Maybe crime does pay. This is a nice place for a podcaster.'

'She worked as an investigative journalist for twenty years and has written several books,' Seb reminded her.

During their research, they'd discovered that Ali Simmons was a forty-two-year-old former journalist who now ran a popular podcast called *Search for Justice*. It had been going for several years and covered everything from murder to extortion, all in a no-nonsense, well-rounded approach that had won many fans.

'True, and I'm keeping an open mind and am willing to hear what she has to say about the case she's building on Helen's murder,' Birdie assured him.

'Who are you trying to convince?' Seb asked, arching his

eyebrow in the particular way he did when he was calling her out on something.

'Ha, ha. Very funny. You know I really want this case. It's been eighteen months since we helped Lady Angelica Charing find the son she'd had adopted when she was only sixteen. Since then, nothing we've done has really piqued my interest. That's why I'm hoping this turns out to be something we can get our teeth into. Is that a crime?'

'Not at all. Like you, I'm keeping an open mind. If Wes Brackstone was falsely imprisoned, I understand Daryl's need to clear his name.'

Birdie nodded. While Seb was the more pragmatic of the two of them, he did share her passion for justice and had excellent instincts.

They walked down the path until reaching the entrance, and Seb pressed the intercom, announced their arrival and they were buzzed in. There was a lift, which Birdie ignored and headed for the stairwell in the far corner. Yes, she could get in one if she had to, but much preferred to take the stairs. Plus, it was a good way to get in some extra cardio, especially now it was cricket season. She took them two at a time and was nicely warm by the time they reached the third floor.

Ali Simmons was waiting by her front door, dressed in jeans and a white T-shirt. Her straight brown hair was hanging loose over her shoulders, and her dark eyes were serious.

'Seb and Birdie, nice to meet you. Come in.' Her smile was warm, and she gestured for them to follow her inside. The apartment wasn't large, but the exposed brick walls, high ceilings and hardwood floors gave it an airy feeling. Birdie tried not to be jealous as they passed an open-plan kitchen through to the sitting room. 'Take a seat. Would you like a hot drink?'

'Thanks. Coffee, if you have it.' Birdie sat down on a long grey sofa that ran under the window.

'No coffee for me, thanks,' Seb said. 'I'm limiting myself to one a day or it plays havoc with my sleep.'

'That's your age,' Birdie said with a grin, but Seb didn't react. Was she becoming too predictable in her teasing?

'I know the feeling,' Ali responded. 'I'm strictly no caffeine after lunch. Would you like a peppermint tea?' Ali padded over to the small kitchen and flicked the switch on the kettle.

'That would be lovely, thank you,' Seb replied.

'Did you have any problems finding a parking spot?' Ali asked as she made the drinks.

'No, there were plenty,' Seb replied.

They sat in silence until Ali returned with the drinks and a plate of chocolate-chip biscuits. Like her podcast persona, her manner was calm and confident. Birdie liked her.

'What would you like to know?' Ali asked as she picked up her mug and took a sip.

'First of all, why did you decide to investigate Helen's murder? Were you already familiar with the case?'

Their research had found plenty of mentions of the crime from old newspaper articles at the time, but not nearly as much online chatter from podcasters and true-crime fans in recent years. Nor had it been revisited either by the police or the media, which meant that apart from the headlines, Birdie hadn't been able to find out much more than she already knew. That part didn't worry her, since she only did a surface skim, but it did raise the question of why a podcaster would be looking into it.

'I didn't come across the Brackstone murder until ten years ago when I was working as an investigative journalist. I was covering the Nicholas Dalton retrial. After Nick was exonerated, I interviewed him, and Wes Brackstone's name came up. They were in the same prison. Dalton claimed that Brackstone had also been wrongly convicted. At the time, I didn't investigate further, but when I saw in the media that Brackstone died last year, it reminded me of Dalton's words and I decided to take a look.'

'I remember the retrial,' Seb said. 'It took eight years for the appeal to go through, and there were multiple errors, including an unreliable witness and proof that Dalton's height and distinct limp didn't match the physical description that multiple witnesses had given.'

'Impressive.' Ali gave him an admiring look, and Birdie bit back a smile. She always enjoyed seeing people react to Seb's super memory. 'What drew me to it was not only the lack of press the case gained, but how the police clammed up any time they were questioned. Something didn't seem right, and so I dug deeper.'

'Except not everyone is innocent, and the police don't always get it wrong,' Seb reminded her.

Birdie had seen numerous people buckle under his calm but astute observations. Not Ali, who merely dipped her head in acknowledgement.

'I agree,' she said. 'I'm not interested in broadcasting episodes based on speculation. I spend a lot of time researching before deciding whether to progress an investigation. I not only have to be mindful of the time it will take, but also of the impact it can have on the victims' families and friends.'

It was a good answer, and Birdie could see why Daryl had agreed to speak with the podcaster after all this time.

'So what did you uncover?' Birdie asked.

'The speed with which Wes Brackstone was arrested concerned me. It was clear the police were looking for a fast way to close the case, which they did in a few days.' Ali held up her hands. 'I know you're both ex-force, and I'm not suggesting that's how things are always done. But there was less transparency back then, and it was easier to hide bad practice. In this case, I discovered that the police had previously been called out to the property for a possible domestic-violence incident.'

'Daryl didn't mention that,' Birdie said, surprised by the omission. She exchanged a glance with Seb.

'No charges were ever brought, but I suspect that's why Wes was on their radar.'

'I'm curious how you discovered this,' Seb said.

'I have a source – who I can't disclose. Suffice to say, I've worked with them for years, and completely trust their information. Though... what's more concerning is what I uncovered in my own research. Helen was a member of The Equality Collective. Or TEC for short. They were a group of radicals committed to fighting corruption in business and she was an active member. Yet that was never investigated.'

'I've never heard of them. Are they still around?' Birdie asked.

Ali shook her head. 'No, they disbanded in 1999. They were well known in the eighties. I found several incidents when going through the newspaper reports about the trial. I'm not saying that her membership in the group was a factor, but surely the police should've looked into it?'

'Totally,' Birdie agreed.

'I've also studied the court records and spoken to Wes's original solicitor. He's retired now, but has kept records of all his cases and gave me full access,' Ali added.

'Impressive,' Birdie admitted.

'It's what I'm trained to do. It's also why I contacted Daryl. While there are mixed opinions on true-crime shows and how they can re-traumatise those affected, I won't do an investigation without approaching all parties and giving them a chance to contribute.'

'If she'd refused, would you have stopped your investigation?' Seb shifted on the sofa to give himself more room. It was a valid question, and Birdie turned to study Ali's face. But her open expression didn't change.

'No. I spend a lot of time deciding whether to take on a case, and everything I've uncovered has convinced me that Wes was innocent. I believe the real killer escaped justice. I have recorded five episodes, but they're not scheduled to be broadcast until mid-August.'

'Why wait?' Seb asked.

'I've taken the case as far as I can in terms of my research and investigative skills. Plus, it's not scheduled until August because I'm halfway through airing another case.'

'So not because you wanted Daryl to hire us and pay for the investigation? To save you the time?' Birdie asked, the thought popping into her head.

'Absolutely not.' Ali met her unflinching gaze with impressive calm. 'I don't promise my listeners any kind of outcome. Besides, it would make your investigation much easier if my episodes weren't yet live. Otherwise, the online chatter and interest could make it difficult.'

It was a good point. If they had to battle well-meaning civilians armed with smartphones and wild theories, it could easily send potential witnesses underground or tamper with evidence.

'Sorry. I shouldn't have implied you were being unscrupulous.' Birdie's shoulders relaxed, and she leant back in the sofa.

'It's understandable and, if I'm honest, I wasn't sure it was worth Daryl's while to pay for a private investigator. Because while you might clear Wes's name, it won't change the fact that he died in prison.'

'And now?' Birdie asked, interested in finding out whether her view had changed.

Ali's serious eyes softened. 'Now I think she might have made a good choice. After you called, I did some research and you've been involved in some impressive cases. I can see you both have integrity.' She smiled. 'I don't think we're so different.'

'Does that mean you'll share your research and the name of

your informant if we take on this case?' Seb asked, leaning forward.

'I won't reveal my source, but I'm prepared to share my research on the condition that you return the favour. Whatever you find, you'll give me access to it before the media is involved.'

'That's reasonable,' Birdie said, standing. 'We still have a few things to discuss before making our final decision. We'll be back in touch soon. Thanks for your help.'

Ali walked them to the door. 'I like Daryl a lot and it's clear how much her mother's death and father's imprisonment affected her. If there's a chance you can find answers to the questions my research raised, I'll be happy.'

Seb and Birdie waited until they were out of the apartment building before speaking.

'What do you think? Are you convinced she's legitimate?' Birdie asked as they made their way to the car. Despite the sun, it was breezy, and she buttoned up her light coat, cursing the perilous British summer.

'I am. It seems I was the one who needed to keep an open mind.' Seb gave her a rueful smile. 'But there are so many of these click-bait shows and articles that are only interested in followers and the like.'

'I agree. But Ali Simmons seems to be exactly what it says on the tin: an investigative journalist who wants justice. She's also saved us a lot of initial legwork.' When they reached the car, Seb unlocked it and Birdie scrambled in, pleased to be out of the breeze. 'I think we should consider taking on the case.'

'I concur. We'll draw up a contract, call Daryl, and ask her to come to the office.' He started the engine and glanced at the time on the dashboard. 'That is, unless you want to stop somewhere to eat first. That's what usually happens when we visit Leicester.'

'You know what they say? When in Leicester, one should always... have lunch.' Birdie grinned as Seb pulled off in the direction of one of her favourite pubs. She could almost taste their 'to die for' fish and chips already.

As Seb navigated the traffic, a wave of nervous excitement went through Birdie. When she'd first joined Seb in the business, she'd been worried they wouldn't get enough cases to hold her interest and support her financially. But she'd been wrong on both counts. And while they had a full workload, there were still certain cases that she knew would take all their skill and focus. The excitement in her stomach told her that this might be one of them.

THREE

Wednesday, 16 July

'Thank you for meeting me so early,' Daryl said at seven-thirty the following morning as she climbed out of her car and walked over to where Birdie had parked in her usual spot outside the front of Rendall Hall. 'There's an important meeting at work and I don't want to be late.' There was a little more colour in the other woman's face, and the look of trepidation from earlier in the week had gone.

'It's not a problem.'

Birdie slung her workbag over one shoulder, and together they headed to the front door. She didn't bother to mention the numerous alarms she'd set herself to make sure she left the house on time and didn't miss the appointment. Birdie was rubbish at timekeeping, but since becoming her own boss, she'd found a system that worked... at least most of the time. It also helped that her brothers were home from university and had part-time jobs that seemed to involve slamming every door in the house as they got ready.

Seb, early riser that he was, would no doubt already be at his desk, so after unlocking the front door, Birdie led Daryl down the wide hallway through to the office. As predicted, Seb was there, and on the table was not only a tea pot but also a plate of fresh muffins. Her stomach rumbled in appreciation. He obviously realised she would've missed breakfast to make sure she got there on time.

'Nice to see you, Daryl,' Seb said, smiling at their visitor.

'Thanks. Sorry for wanting to be here so early. The last week of the school term is chaotic enough, and it isn't helped by the head calling an early meeting before the pupils arrive. Not that much work is done this week – the children are way too excited about the summer holidays for them to concentrate.' Daryl took a seat, placing her large handbag on the floor.

'It must be like herding cats,' Seb said. 'My niece is ten, and despite how much she loves school, even she's getting excited.'

Birdie sat next to her, while Seb poured three cups of tea.

The rich aroma filled the office as he handed Daryl a cup. She took it but waved away the offer of a muffin. Birdie didn't follow her lead and instead took a bite of the one she'd taken. Blueberries and cinnamon danced on her tongue and helped her feel more awake. She gave her partner a grateful smile.

'We met with Ali Simmons yesterday,' Seb said once he was settled in his seat. 'And after going through some of her initial research, we agree there are grounds to warrant further investigation. If it's what you wish, we will take the case.'

There was silence as a mix of emotions crossed Daryl's face. Finally, she let out a relieved sigh.

'Thank you. It wasn't until after we'd met on Monday that I realised how important this is to me.'

Birdie, who'd embarked on finding her birth parents several years ago, could relate. It had been like an unanswered question permanently floating around the edges of her mind. And while she hadn't yet contacted her birth father, she had established a good relationship with her birth mother and half-sisters. More importantly, the hollowness and uncertainty no longer plagued her. It was a welcome relief.

Of course, it didn't always work out like that. Which was why they had to be cautious regarding what they promised their clients.

'It's important for you to understand that what we discover might not be what you were hoping for,' Birdie said.

'I'm prepared for that,' Daryl said, her jaw set firm. 'What happens now?'

'We need to go through our contract, but before we do, we have a few questions for you to get us started.' Birdie retrieved her notebook from the desk, where she'd left it the previous evening. Seb, with his super memory, didn't need to write anything down, but she did. It also helped her to focus. 'Please could you tell us about your parents' marriage? Ali mentioned the police had been called out to your house on the suspicion of domestic abuse, but no charge was brought.'

A shadow crossed Daryl's face before she nodded.

'That's correct. But it was something and nothing. My parents were both good people, and I loved them dearly. And they loved each other, too. But we were on a street where everyone knew everyone else's business. It was a neighbour who called the police when they overheard a loud argument between the two of them. I'm still not sure why she decided to intervene.'

'Our street was the same. Still is,' Birdie admitted. It was one of the benefits and disadvantages of growing up in the same place. 'Can you remember what the argument was over?' Birdie asked.

'Money. But not as you might think. My dad was a civil engineer and worked for a big company in Leicester. He rarely talked about his job, but now I realise he was well paid. We were comfortably off, and I don't remember ever wanting for anything. That was the problem for my mum. She hated that we had so much money. Felt guilty, even. She studied sociology at university and had strong views on social inequality. When she wasn't working, she was always going to meetings and volunteering. She wanted to help those who couldn't help themselves.'

Daryl broke off and dabbed at her eyes with a tissue that she pulled out from her pocket.

'I know it's painful to revisit old memories, but the more we know about your mum and dad, the better,' Birdie said, already having a much clearer picture of what Helen Brackstone was like when she was alive.

'Are you able to continue?' Seb asked, taking over.

'Yes.' Daryl nodded.

'You mentioned that your mother worked.'

'Yes. Once I started school, Mum wanted to work full-time, but Dad thought it would be better for her to be part-time so she was around during the holidays or if I was off sick. So she started working for a charity that ran a food bank to help feed the local homeless. It wasn't such a well-known concept back then, and she spent a lot of time convincing people to donate food every day, instead of just at Christmas. She was passionate about it and often roped me in – not to mention my friends – to sort through all the canned goods. We often helped her to do street appeals, too. I was happy to help and proud of what she was doing.'

'She sounds very dedicated,' Birdie said. 'You mentioned that your mother often went out to meetings. Did she talk about them at all?'

'No.' The brightness in Daryl's eyes faded. 'Ali mentioned The Equality Collective, and I've been wracking my mind but have no memory of her having anything to do with them. Nearly everything she talked about involved the food bank. As far as the meetings were concerned, all I know is that she would regularly go out at night.'

'How often would that be?'

'Sometimes once a week, but every now and then, she would be out every night.'

'Did she say where she was going?'

'No, but I'd assumed it was to do with the food bank. But that might not be true. She might have been doing stuff with this Equality Collective organisation. But I have no idea what.'

Birdie caught Seb's eye. They'd started researching TEC yesterday afternoon, but hadn't found a huge amount of information.

'After your father was arrested, what happened then? Did you move in with relatives? Move away from Market Harborough altogether?'

There was silence as Daryl stared at the wall, as if it were a movie screen. Was she watching her old life play out once again?

'Mum's sister, Aunt Kerry, was my only relation, and she agreed to take care of me. One of the social workers suggested that she move into our house, but I couldn't face sleeping there after what happened, so I moved into her flat. But it was tiny, because she lived alone – she was a nurse and had never married. After the trial, we decided to move back to our house and I've been there ever since, apart from when I went to university.'

'Does Kerry still live with you?' Birdie asked. They'd like to interview the woman if they could.

'No. She died six years after my mum of breast cancer. I was only twenty when it happened and it totally gutted me. She was such a lovely woman, and even though she was so different from Mum, we were very close.' Daryl glanced away, once again lost in memory.

Birdie swallowed. Both sisters had died far too early. No wonder Daryl seemed shrouded in sadness.

'I'm sorry to hear that. Were you ever tempted to move away and start a new life elsewhere?' Birdie asked.

For the first time, Daryl gave a hint of a smile. 'Only every other day. But that was partly because I was a young teacher at the time and had some challenging students. Maybe if I'd met the right person, I would have done. As it was, it was only ever me and now my daughter – her father was never on the scene. Financially, it made sense to stay in the house. I know that some people might find it gruesome, but for me, it means that, in a way, both my parents got to see Olivia grow up. Of course, she's completely different to me. While I stayed put, Olivia went travelling and met Max. They're married now and live in Dorset, along with my two beautiful grandchildren.'

'You must be looking forward to seeing them during the school holidays,' Birdie said.

'Very much. I was thinking of moving down there. But the houses are way more expensive and after meeting Ali, I decided that I'd rather invest my savings in finding out the truth. My daughter understands and is fully behind my decision.'

'We'd like to interview people who knew your mum and dad back then. Friends or family. Can you give us some names, please?' Birdie asked.

'We're a very small family. I'm an only child, so was my dad, and Mum only had Kerry. Some of the neighbours are still living there, but I wouldn't call them close friends of my parents. Oh... Hang on... There's Carla Brinkworth. I forgot about her. She went to university with Mum and still keeps in contact. Mainly birthday and Christmas cards. I can give you her details.'

Daryl pulled out her phone and scrolled through the screen before reading out a phone number and address. Birdie jotted it down, and then they spent the next ten minutes going over the contract and undertaking the administrative tasks involved with taking on a new client.

Once everything was sorted, they escorted Daryl to the front door and watched as she drove off down the long drive. So far, they didn't have much to go on, and only limited access to information. But, like all new cases, they would have to follow the evidence to see what turned up.

FOUR

Thursday, 17 July

'Has anyone seen my phone charger?' Keira asked the following morning as she peered into the office.

Her long hair was already washed and dried and she was wearing a new dress that Seb suspected his mother – who had formed a close bond with Keira over the last eighteen months – had bought her.

'How can you lose a charger? Isn't that what your highly superior autobiographical memory's for?' Birdie said, looking up from her computer, a fake innocent expression plastered across her face.

Seb's daughter had inherited his talent – or curse, depending on the way you looked at it – and Birdie was fond of teasing them about it.

'Yes. But while I remember where I put it, I have no idea why it's no longer there,' Keira retorted before gesturing at Birdie's own phone, which was currently plugged into a charger. She placed a hand on her hip and smirked. 'Case closed.'

'Oh. Sorry. I thought it was mine.' Birdie wrinkled her nose and disconnected it. 'Here you are. You can use it while we get you up to speed.'

'I'll get you a spare charger for your birthday, and then you can leave mine alone.' Keira grinned, plugged in her own phone, and then dragged over a chair, positioning it between the two desks.

When Keira had first arrived on Seb's doorstep, at age seventeen, she'd been keen to help with cases. Although he'd been willing, he wasn't sure her enthusiasm would last. But he'd been wrong; not only had she continued to help, but she'd also finished her first year at the University of Birmingham, studying psychology and criminology. She'd received excellent grades and Seb couldn't be prouder, not least because it was recognised as a top university in that discipline. Plus, it was clear by her enthusiasm and sharp questioning that she had a genuine interest in the area. She'd mentioned on several occasions that after her course, she intended to study for a master's in forensic psychology.

It didn't take them long to go through their recent case load and once they'd finished, Keira's dark eyes gleamed with excitement.

'O.M.G. You met Ali Simmons? I *love* that podcast. I listen to it all the time. What's she like? Is she awesome?' Keira demanded before catching herself. 'Ignore me. I'll stop fangirling so we can get on with the case. What's the plan? Would you like me to start researching? Or... I could go into the field with you?'

Seb bit back a smile at his daughter's persistence. 'As I've already explained to you, there are inherent risks in the work we do, that Birdie and I have been trained to look out for and deal with.'

'But not everything you do is risky,' Keira persisted. 'Sometimes it's just asking questions.'

'That is true, but equally we can't predict when things are going to turn. Maybe in the future we will allow you to accompany us, but not yet,' he said, kindly, not wanting to hurt her feelings. 'Besides, in this case first we need to discover more about the original investigation, which means all of us undertaking research.'

The mounting shadows on Keira's face swept away and she nodded. 'I love going down research rabbit holes, as you know. What about police records? Is there any chance we can access them?'

'Unfortunately, that will be almost impossible, because it's a closed case. Most records are destroyed after seven years,' he told her.

'While Keira does some internet research, I'll head down to the police station and talk to Twiggy. I'll text first to make sure he's there. Even if the records have been destroyed, he might remember the case. After all, he's even older than you, Seb,' Birdie said, with a smirk.

This earnt a snicker from Keira, and Seb sighed, deciding not to comment. Instead, he nodded.

'Good idea,' he said. 'While you do that, I'll follow up on Carla Brinkworth, Helen's friend, and arrange an interview. I'll also look at Helen and Wes's finances… if there's anything available.'

'Great. Keira, Ali has sent over her research. I'll forward it to you if you want to start going through it for us.' Birdie tapped away at her keyboard before getting to her feet and heading to the door.

Once she was gone, Keira pulled a slim laptop out of her bag. But instead of moving over to Birdie's unoccupied desk, she stayed in her chair, fiddling with a strand of long hair.

It was a habit she had when something was on her mind.

'How about we make a coffee before we start and you can fill me in on the visit with your grandparents?' Seb stood up and headed towards the kitchen, closely followed by his daughter, who seemed eager for his company.

Had something happened in London?

While he was late to the parenting game, he'd begun to fully appreciate how tricky it could be, and since she'd come into his life, there'd been a couple of sleepless nights when she'd gone out to parties with her new friends and hadn't arrived home until after three in the morning. It was nothing he hadn't done at the same age, but it had given him a new appreciation for his own parents and their nerves of steel.

Then there had been the anniversary of her mother Melanie's death. That had been tough. Seb hadn't seen Melanie since they'd parted ways the day after they graduated; but Keira had struggled on the day and all Seb could do was stand by, unsure how to support her.

'It was brilliant. Grandpa got a little annoyed that I beat him at chess, but I told him it was much better for me to do that than to let him win. Granny agreed. Not that she told him that, of course. She just did that serene smile of hers. Let's see, what else? We went to see three musicals. You would have loved them. Plus, the shopping was awesome. As well as this dress, I got two pairs of shoes and the cutest bikini. Which reminds me, I must call Lucy about going for a day trip to the lake. She was telling me about it before we broke up for summer. Oh, and Uncle Hubert said to say hello. He had a meeting in London and called in to see us. You'll never guess what? He's started doing yoga, which is cool.' The words tumbled out of Keira at a rate of knots.

Seb made them both a hot drink as his daughter continued, and they retreated to the sunny part of the kitchen where the sunlight flooded in.

'Yoga? Hubert?' he said, while wondering how long it would be before she roped him into trying it. Still, at least it meant whatever was bothering her didn't involve his family.

'I know. Weird, right? But so good for him because of his mental health issue.'

'You know about that?' Seb hadn't mentioned it to his daughter.

'He told me. He said that it's good to let people know when you have issues to deal with.'

Never would he have imagined Hubert confiding in Keira.

'He's right and I hope you realise the same goes between you and me. Are you going to tell me the problem?'

'Who says there is one?' Keira asked, toying with another long strand of hair. Sighing, she ceased fidgeting. 'Okay, there *is* something I want to ask you... I was hoping you'd call George for me.'

Seb frowned. Dr Georgina Cavendish was a friend. She lectured in forensic psychology at Lenchester University, and he'd met her several years ago while helping DCI Whitney Walker on a case. Last year, George had given Keira some career guidance and they'd got on well.

'Do you have a problem with your course?'

'No, it's nothing bad. Though it's understandable you might think that. It's called a negativity bias. We're hardwired to respond more to negative stimuli, and in turn, it can make us expect the worst,' she reassured him kindly.

Seb smiled at what Birdie called 'Fresher Alert' every time Keira gave them a nugget of wisdom. Apparently, Birdie's two brothers were the same.

'So, what's this about?'

'It's about the course. I know taking a double degree will give me more flexibility career-wise, but I don't think that's necessary because I know exactly what I want to do. There's so much theory to learn, and although it's interesting, it's hard to stay focused when it's not directly relevant. You get what I mean, don't you?'

Unfortunately, he did. While having their memory made

certain parts of education easier, it also came with its own challenges. Like staying focused when they weren't sufficiently challenged.

'Where does George fit into this all?'

'I want to transfer to Lenchester and do a straight forensic psychology degree,' she said in a rush. 'And it's not just because I'm bored. It's the area I want to work in. It's all so fascinating. I read one of her papers last month and it was brilliant. I think I could learn so much from her... and the rest of the lecturers, of course.'

Seb ran a hand through his hair. Part of him was relieved that it wasn't anything serious, but he still wasn't convinced about the idea.

'Have you thought through the implications? Even if you are able to receive some cross-credit for modules you've already undertaken, you might still have to repeat some... especially if they're mandatory.'

'That's why I want to speak with George to see what she thinks.' Keira's face coloured. 'I was going to call her myself – she did give me her number – but then I chickened out. She's a bit scary, isn't she? That's why I thought if you called her...'

'At your age, you should be doing this yourself... but between you and me, I too find George a little intimidating, so I'll call her and suggest that we meet up to discuss it.'

'Really? Thanks so much,' Keira said with a relieved smile. 'Can we do it now?'

Seb nodded and brought up George's number. The forensic psychologist answered on the second ring in her usual matter-of-fact manner.

'Sebastian. How may I help?'

'Hello, George. I hope I'm not disturbing you.' Seb put the phone on speaker.

'Of course not. I wouldn't have answered the phone if you

were,' she replied, which made Keira grin. 'Do you need help with a case?'

'No, this isn't work related. Keira and I would like to take you to lunch next week, if you're available. We'd like to discuss her studies.'

'Hmm... Let's see... I can do next Friday if that suits you both.'

Seb glanced over to Keira, who gave him two thumbs up. He smiled. 'That would be perfect.'

'Shall I invite Whitney? I'm sure she'd like to see you.'

'That's an excellent idea,' he agreed.

'Very well then. It's come at a pertinent time because I spoke to one of Keira's lecturers recently, at a conference, and she informed me that although Keira's an exceptional student, she isn't pushing herself. We should discuss this because I have no time for people who waste their talent.'

Seb said his goodbyes and finished the call. Keira's face was bright with excitement as she stood up and hugged him.

'Did you hear that? George thinks I have talent.'

'She also thinks you need to push yourself more.'

'Which is why I want to move to Lenchester. Because then, I will. Promise. I can't wait until next Friday.'

'I'm afraid you'll have to. Remember, this isn't a foregone conclusion. We're at discussion stage only. Now, can we get back to work?'

'Yes. I'm going to research TEC like crazy.' Keira stopped to hug Elsa, who had appeared in the doorway, her brown eyes full of questions about what they were doing. 'Once I've finished, I'll take this one for a walk.'

Elsa seemed to accept this, and his daughter and dog disappeared back into the office. Seb quickly tidied the kitchen up and followed them. He had his own research to undertake.

FIVE

Thursday, 17 July

Market Harborough Police Station was built for function rather than style. All the same, Birdie gave the dull brickwork a fond pat as she stepped back into her old workplace. Her ex-partner, Neil 'Twiggy' Branch, was sitting at the front desk, his unruly brown hair had streaks of grey in it, but apart from that, he didn't look any different from when they were last together.

'Someone pinch me.' He glanced at the old wall clock and then at the watch on his wrist. 'You're five minutes early and don't look like you got dressed in the dark.'

'Well, you don't look like Sarge has stuck you on the night shift recently, so you must be behaving yourself,' she retorted, before putting down the two coffees she'd bought on the way over to give him a long hug. After a moment, he made a grumbling noise and pulled away.

'All right. No need to get soppy or anything. I told you in my text that I'm fine. The doctor's happy with everything and so is my occupational therapist.'

'Good to hear,' Birdie said. When he was diagnosed with

frontotemporal dementia, it had hit her hard. It was the first time someone close to her had had a serious illness. But she also knew how much Twiggy hated people fussing over him, so she held up her hands up. 'And you can relax. No more spontaneous hugs for at least a month.'

'Promises, promises,' he joked. 'It's good to see you remembered how terrible our coffee is here.' Twiggy nodded at the takeaway cups.

'Trust me, the burnt cardboard taste will be with me forever.' She passed him one of the cups. 'Don't worry, I got you decaf with no sugar, so Evie won't hunt me down.'

'You don't want to get on her bad side,' Twiggy agreed, referring to his wife, his eyes twinkling with pride. 'How's that partner of yours?' he added but no longer with malice.

When Birdie first started helping Seb with cases, Twiggy had been jealous, thinking that he was losing his partner. But once Birdie left the force to join CIS the two of them came to an easy-*ish* truce.

'He's fine thanks.'

'Let's go upstairs. Sarge is out, Rambo and Tiny are on a training course, and the new guy's in court.'

'New guy?'

'Sparkle's replacement.'

'Interesting they didn't ever replace me,' Birdie mused.

'No one could fill your shoes... in so many ways,' Twiggy teased. 'Not to mention the budget cuts have been crippling. Anyway, let's not go into that or I'll be sounding like Sarge.'

They walked past the ancient lift, to the staircase, which took them to the open-plan office. Her old desk seemed to have become a dumping ground for folders, boxes of plastic gloves, face masks, and several abandoned cups. To be fair, though, it didn't look much different from when she'd been there. An unexpected wave of nostalgia hit her. She was going to be thirty this year, and if anyone had told her five years ago that she'd end up being a private investigator, she'd have laughed in their face.

'Come on then, what's this about?' Twiggy asked, dragging over a second chair so they could both sit at his desk. He took the lid off the coffee cup and blew on it, before taking a sip.

'We've been hired to investigate the Helen Brackstone murder. She lived in Market Harborough and was killed in—'

'1989,' he cut in, eyes wide with surprise as he put the cup down.

'That's right,' Birdie agreed, her mouth pursed. 'That was quick. I take it you remember the case?'

'It's a hard one to forget. I was at school in Northampton and our football team was due to play the school her daughter went to on the day it happened. The match was cancelled, obviously, but we were all shocked. There was so much publicity in the newspapers, all of them trying to get photos of her, the poor thing. It was disgusting.'

'Agreed.' Birdie had already found enough of the old articles to have seen the sensationalist photographs plastered across the front pages. There was no consideration for the fact that their client had been a schoolgirl at the time. 'It's the daughter, Daryl Brackstone, who hired us. She's always believed her father was innocent and wants us to find out the truth.'

Twiggy leant back in his chair and gave a low whistle. 'That's a big ask, but I get it if she thinks her dad was innocent. You know, Daryl Brackstone taught both my girls. She was an excellent teacher and they loved her, but she always seemed to have an air of melancholy about her.'

'*Melancholy?* Since when do you use fancy words like that?' Birdie raised an eyebrow.

'Fine.' Twiggy grinned. 'I thought she looked sad, but Evie said it was melancholy. So, why now?'

Although it was the same question she and Seb had asked Daryl, Birdie didn't want to mention the upcoming podcasts, or the fact that Ali thought the police hadn't done their due diligence. Instead, she simply shrugged.

'I guess it's a matter of being able to afford it.'

'Fair enough. Question is, what do you want from me? I doubt the case records will still be here. Records aren't usually kept that long'

'I know it's a long shot. But could you check?'

'I can, but you know that even if they're here, you can't have them. Everything taken out is logged.'

'Let's see if they exist first,' Birdie said, cajoling. For once, Twiggy didn't need any convincing and he turned on his computer. While he began his search, Birdie checked her messages. There were several from estate agents, wanting to know what she thought of some of the houses and apartments she'd visited, and one from Annie, the wicket keeper on her cricket team.

> Anyone up for drinks after the match on Saturday? It's my twenty-fifth birthday and I need to commiserate – not to mention getting raging drunk. There could even be dancing. Who's with me? Annie xoxo

Birdie grinned. She might not get raging drunk anymore, but she still loved a good night out, and it would help distract her from the dire housing market. She quickly replied.

> Count me in.

'I know that look. What are you planning?' Twiggy demanded, and Birdie put down her phone.

'Nothing but a bit of innocent relaxation after the game on Saturday. No doubt we'll be celebrating another spectacular win, thanks to my bowling.' She winked before leaning closer to the screen. 'Well? Any joy?'

'No, I'm afraid not. Still, it saves us from having to argue over it,' he replied.

'We don't argue, we have creative discussions,' she corrected him, frowning. 'What about who worked the case? Is that on record?'

'Yes, and it's not good news. DI Best was the senior investigating officer, but he died a long time ago. The only other one on the team was Jeff Dunbar. He was a DC back then. He retired twelve years ago, a detective sergeant. And good riddance, because he was nothing but trouble.' Twiggy's mouth turned down in a scowl.

Birdie's stomach dropped.

'Was he really that bad?' she asked, the sinking sensation in her stomach not going away. Had Ali Simmons been right?

'Damn straight he was,' Twiggy growled. 'He was always cutting corners and wouldn't think twice about throwing someone under the bus if it would make him look good. Even Sarge cracked a smile the day he left. Who knew the old boy had it in him?'

'You might not want to let him hear you say that.' Birdie bit back a smile. And people called *her* impulsive. 'Do you think Dunbar would interfere with a case?'

'Dunbar would do just about anything. I'm convinced he was on the take, but there was never any evidence. It was one of those gut feelings that wouldn't go away.'

'I know exactly what you mean,' Birdie said. 'Dunbar's the perfect place to start. Do you have his contact details, by any chance?'

'Hang on, let's see.' Twiggy turned back to his screen and scrolled through several pages, and then wrote down something on a piece of paper. He passed it over. 'Here's the address and phone number. He lives in Wilby.'

'I know the place.' Birdie slipped the paper into her pocket. 'Thanks, Twig. I do have one more question. Have you heard ever of a group called The Equality Collective? Helen was a member back in the day.'

'The name sounds familiar, but I don't know why...'

The door opened and Sarge walked in. At the sight of Birdie, his pale-blue eyes crinkled and he raised an eyebrow. 'Well, you're a sight for sore eyes. This place has been far too quiet lately.'

'I bet you never thought you'd hear yourself say that. You're looking well, Sarge.'

'No, I'm not,' he retorted. 'My back hurts, my cholesterol is through the roof, and someone nicked my parking spot this morning.'

'And yet you're smiling. Why's that? Because you've seen me?' she asked as he joined them at the desk.

In the past, he'd always been in a hurry, but he seemed to have mellowed as he got closer to retirement. Not that she knew exactly when that would be.

'Yeah... something like that,' he replied, though a hint of a smile tugged at his mouth. 'What brings you to our neck of the woods? No investigations of your own keeping you occupied? You never did like sitting still for long.'

'Don't worry. We have more than enough work to keep us busy. We're working on an old case and I'm looking for background information. Do you remember the Helen Brackstone case?'

The smile faded. 'I do. I was a young police constable at the time. There was a lot of media attention, and the bigwigs wanted the case closed quickly. As I remember they only ever considered her husband for the murder. Hardly surprising with Best and Dunbar on the case. I take it Twiggy's already told you that?'

Birdie nodded. 'I was hoping you might know about The Equality Collective. They were around at the time. Did you ever come across them?'

'Now that's a name I haven't heard in a while.' He rubbed his chin, as if trying to force out a memory. 'They caused their fair share of problems, that's for sure. They were based out of Leicester, I believe, but had a habit of popping up all over the place if there was a cause they wanted to support. They were forever putting up posters and protesting issues.'

'What kind of issues?'

'There seemed to be a range. But mainly involving big companies. I wouldn't call them extremists, as such, but they did extreme things to attract publicity. Like throwing paint over cars, or gluing their hands to the road so they could stop the traffic.'

'Did that ever happen in Market Harborough, and were any of them arrested?'

'If they were, it was only for minor infringements, and there were no repeat arrests. But they certainly skirted on the wrong side of the law.'

'Are they still going?' Birdie asked.

Sarge shook his head. 'I'm almost certain they fizzled out, like a lot of other groups at the time. But I can't be one hundred per cent sure. Why? Do you think they were tied up with this case?'

'We don't know. We've been told Helen was a member, which is why we're looking into them.' Birdie got to her feet. 'Anyway, I'd better let you get on. Thanks so much for the help.'

'Let me know if there's anything else,' Twiggy said, sounding unusually serious. 'If there's been a miscarriage of justice, I want to know about it.'

'Twiggy's right. It might not have happened on our watch... but—' Sarge broke off and gruffly coughed. 'Keep us up to date.'

'Will do,' Birdie promised, pleased that despite their moaning and grumbling, her former colleagues never wavered in their integrity; the idea that there might have been underhanded dealings by one of their own wasn't something they would tolerate.

That made three of them.

The traffic was light as she drove back to East Farndon, stopping first to pick up some lunch for them. There was no sign of Keira's silver car, but Seb was out in the garden. Elsa lazily pawed at a stick a few metres away, as if deciding whether she should pick it up. Birdie jogged across the well-mown grass, pleased to shake out her legs and arms after a morning sitting down.

'How did you get on?' Seb asked as Birdie joined him and Elsa trotted over and nuzzled Birdie's leg.

'Good.' Birdie dropped to her knees and gave the dog a hug, soaking in the soft warmth of her fur as she talked. 'Like we suspected, the case notes have all been destroyed. The SIO on the case is dead, but I have the name and contact details of the DC who worked with him.'

'And?' Seb raised an eyebrow, obviously picking up on her distaste.

'Jeff Dunbar had a reputation as being slippery. He retired before I joined, so I don't know him, but Twiggy and Sarge both do, and neither of them are fans.'

'Not a good recommendation. I can imagine Twiggy clashing with people, but DS Weston always struck me as a good judge of character.'

'You obviously didn't hear him back in the day, when he was bawling me out for being late,' Birdie retorted, but she knew he had a point. While her senior officer might have given her a hard time when she'd been on the force, it was only because he wanted her to reach her full potential. 'You're right about Sarge, though. I might not have liked some of his tactics, but he was always fair, and Twiggy has great instincts.'

'Most of the time,' Seb corrected, obviously remembering

the hard time Birdie's ex-partner had given her current partner at the time. 'Was there anything else?'

'Not really. Twiggy had heard of TEC but didn't know anything about them. Sarge remembered a bit more,' she said, filling him in on the rest of the conversation. 'Have you found any more about them yet?'

'Keira's compiled all of Ali's research for us to read, but had to head out for a dentist appointment. I've been working through Daryl and Wes's finances, but so far nothing seems amiss there. I've also reached out to the rest home in Market Harborough where Carla Brinkworth lives. I haven't yet heard back, but I'm hoping we can arrange an interview. Though, before speaking to her we should question Dunbar. We'll go tomorrow. I want to finish my research.'

'If he's half as bad as Twiggy told me, I don't think we should call ahead in case he tries to get out of it. We should catch him unawares.'

'Agreed,' Seb said as they headed towards the house. 'If there's one thing for sure, retired detectives love talking about the "good old days", so despite his reputation, we might still get something out of him.'

'I hope so.'

Birdie clenched her fist, as if holding a cricket ball. The idea of a bent police officer made her blood boil, but without Dunbar's help, it would be difficult to find out what happened during the investigation.

Talk about being between a rock and a hard place.

SIX

Friday, 18 July

Wilby was a tiny village on the outskirts of Wellingborough, known for its quaint limestone church, dating back to the thirteen hundreds. Seb pulled to a stop outside a small but well-maintained bungalow. The tiny garden was filled with dahlias, which suggested that Jeff Dunbar spent at least part of his retirement tending to them. That didn't mean he wasn't corrupt, though.

Seb peered around, searching for a car outside the property, but there were no signs of one. 'Let's hope he's home. Otherwise, we'll have a wait on our hands.'

'Only one way to find out.' Birdie opened the gate and walked up the short path.

They'd spent the half-hour drive discussing how to approach Dunbar while keeping him on side. They needed his assistance and didn't want him to dig his heels in and refuse to help. Their research hadn't flagged any disciplinary actions that would confirm Twiggy's belief that the ex-officer was corrupt, but that didn't mean he wasn't... Just that he hadn't been caught.

Birdie pressed the plastic buzzer, and the jangling chimes were soon followed by a shuffle of feet before the door swung open. Jeff Dunbar was tall and lean with salt-and-pepper hair and green eyes. He was wearing corduroy trousers and a checked shirt with the sleeves rolled up to his elbows. At seventy-two, he hadn't changed much from the photo Seb had accessed from when he was a serving police officer.

'Yes?' he asked, his shrewd eyes observing them.

His manner was open and curious rather than on guard.

'Hi, I'm Birdie, and this is Sebastian Clifford. We're private investigators and have been asked to investigate the murder of Helen Brackstone.'

If Dunbar was thrown by the question, it didn't show. Instead, he nodded and opened the door wider. 'Well, you've come to the right place. Of course, I was only a DC back then, but it was my first murder investigation, so I remember it well. I presume you've been hired by Wes and Helen's daughter, Daryl. She's the only person who would care.'

'That's correct,' Seb said.

Dunbar led them through to a small lounge. It was neat and tidy, but the lights were turned off, and the only noise came from a battery-powered radio. Did that mean that money was tight?

'Would you like a hot drink?'

'Only if you're having one,' Birdie said, obviously noticing the austere setting as well.

Dunbar shook his head and gestured to an empty cup on the small coffee table, which was next to a half-finished crossword.

'I just finished one.' He sat down on what was clearly his armchair and nodded to the small two-seater across from him.

'But it's nice to have visitors. Most of the time, it's just me and the four walls for company.'

'You're not married?'

'No. I was one of those fools who let the job take over my life. I kept thinking there would be time for that stuff later. You two look like you were once on the force, so I guess you know what I mean.'

'We were, and do,' Seb agreed, not bothering to give him any more details. Dunbar might not be so forthcoming if he knew Birdie had been based at his old station. 'One of the many reasons why we both left. Thank you for agreeing to talk.'

'Not much else to do these days, is there? So, what would you like to know? As far as cases went, it wasn't very challenging. Wes Brackstone wasn't exactly a mastermind criminal.'

'We were hoping you could explain what happened,' Birdie said, her posture visibly stiffening, but Dunbar didn't appear to notice.

'We got the call mid-afternoon from Helen's sister... I can't remember her name.'

'Kerry,' Seb supplied.

'Yes, that's right. Kerry was the one who found her. Said she'd been worried because they'd arranged to meet for lunch and Helen stood her up, which wasn't like her at all. She went to the house, and when no one answered, she used the spare key and let herself in—'

'Where did she get the key from?' Birdie interrupted.

'It was kept under a pot in the garden. You know what it was like then. Most people did the same. Anyway, she found Helen unresponsive in the kitchen and called emergency services. The paramedics turned up and pronounced her dead. The pathologist said it was cyanide poisoning, and lo and behold, that's what we found in the garden shed. At the time, there was a half-drunk cup of coffee on the table, which was later tested to prove that's how she'd ingested the poison.'

'Did the pathologist mention how unlikely it would've been for Helen to knowingly drink a cup of coffee with enough pesticide in to kill her? The taste would've been impossible to disguise,' Birdie asked.

'Yes, but she didn't drink it by accident. Wes was there and forced her to swallow it. It wasn't the first time he'd threatened her. But unfortunately for her, it was the last.'

'What made you so sure that's what he did?' Birdie asked, the pen in her hand hovering over the notebook she was holding.

Dunbar picked at his teeth with his thumbnail before shrugging. 'It wasn't rocket science. It's not like she was going to swallow it of her own accord.' He smirked as if enjoying the memory. 'Also, there were receipts to prove he'd bought the cyanide-laced weed killer the month before, and a neighbour had seen his car parked outside the house earlier in the day. She said he wasn't usually home at that time of day, which is why she noticed it.' He leant back in his chair, spreading his arms across its back like he owned the room. 'Look, we were called out to the house following a fight they'd had, and while she never pressed charges, it was obvious he'd slapped her around a bit.'

Dunbar was clearly trying to colour the story, and the casual way he'd described domestic violence made Seb's stomach turn. Next to him, Birdie had clamped down on her jaw, no doubt trying to conceal her own distaste of the man.

'What about The Equality Collective? Did you investigate Helen's association with them?' Seb asked.

Dunbar rolled his eyes and checked his watch. 'No. Why would we? Helen Brackstone was a suburban housewife with a part-time job and a kid to look after.'

'Yet she attended their meetings every week and was seen at protests,' Seb pushed, silently thanking Ali Simmons for her research.

Dunbar's thin lips twitched, and he let out an exaggerated sigh. 'Okay, we did know about TEC. Wes mentioned it to us, but it was clear he was trying to shift the blame away from him. We didn't buy it.'

'Why not?'

'TEC were chicken feed compared to some of the other groups around at the time. They were a bunch of idealistic students who were hypercritical of middle-class citizens like you and me.' He focused on Seb and narrowed his eyes. 'Well, not you, if the accent's anything to go by. Anyway, it was pathetic. They liked to think they were changing the world, while still going home to their comfortable homes each night. If Helen really believed in all that crap, she wouldn't have been living in that fancy house of hers, while Wes went out every day to work for a company that built industrial machinery.'

'So, it wasn't just a case of you ignoring evidence?' Birdie pressed.

Seb glared at Birdie. *Play it cool.*

But Dunbar's face remained impassive, and he chuckled. 'I know that some cases have more twists and turns than a soap opera, but this wasn't one of them. We weren't ignoring evidence. We were lucky enough to find it without too much trouble.'

'But I'm sure you were careful about being thorough.' Seb kept his tone even, not wanting Dunbar to clam up.

'Yes, of course we did our job properly.'

'Did you keep your old notebooks, by any chance? Because we'd love to get a bit more insight into how the case unfolded,' Birdie asked, plastering an unnatural smile on her face.

But it appeared to work, because Dunbar responded with a toothy smile. Seb got the distinct feeling that the retired detective considered himself a ladies man. He bit back a chuckle at the thought of Birdie being interested in the man.

'I do. Not that I've looked at them in years. I probably won't be able to read my own writing because everything was written down in a rush.'

'Tell me about it. Mine's crap, too. Still, we'd like to see them, if that's okay,' Birdie went along, though her knee was jiggling: a clear indication that it was not easy for her to play nice.

There was silence before Dunbar finally raised himself from the chair.

'Sure. But all you can do is read them. You're not to take notes or photos, and you can't take them away with you. I'm not taking any chances. If they end up in the wrong hands, they'll be published on the internet or sold on eBay. You hear about that happening all the time.'

'We understand,' Birdie said, placing her notebook and pen on the table to indicate she was happy to comply. With Seb's memory, there was no need to take them away, or write down notes. He only had to read something once and it was 'in the vault' as one of his teachers had said. That wasn't exactly how he'd describe the process, but he didn't correct people if that was what they believed.

The retired officer returned ten minutes later and placed a cardboard box on the coffee table before settling back into his chair. 'That's all of them. The years are written on the covers. Help yourself.'

Birdie dropped down to her knees and lifted out a large pile of familiar-looking notebooks. They did tend to vary between forces, but there was a familiarity to them that prompted Seb to recall his own collection. Despite his memory, he'd always kept notebooks during his time on the force, so they could be used in court and also be evidence for his continuing professional development.

It didn't take Birdie long to divide them into several piles before returning to the sofa with two books. One of which she handed to Seb. It was dated the year of Helen's murder.

Dunbar's handwriting was small and tight and had faded over time, but by the third line, Seb had managed to decode the compacted letters. He flicked through the dates until he reached 15 May.

The notes were not what he would call methodical. There was no mention of the address or even who the victim was. Further on was the interview with the neighbour.

Rosemary Fry, 39 YO. The neighbour from 18 Northampton Road said that.

The text broke off and several lines had been crossed out so thoroughly that they were hardly visible. It went against one of the tenets of not removing anything from the book, and it highlighted to Seb how the retired detective worked.

It picked up again further down the page.

Fry saw Wes Brackstone's car – F Reg Rover – parked in the driveway at 9.30 a.m. when she looked out her front window. It was unusual for him to have not left for work, which is why she noticed it. He left an hour later and didn't return until after the body had been discovered.

Seb thought back. F reg would have meant that the car would've been under a year old, and he had to admit, it did prove Dunbar's theory that whatever Helen's political leanings were, her lifestyle was very middle class. Still, it hardly made Wes a guilty man. There had been no mention of the tree that Daryl told them would have obstructed Rosemary's view of the driveway.

He continued to read, wanting to read the interview with Wes Brackstone, but there wasn't one. All that was included were the results of several more interviews. One with Helen's sister, Kerry, who found the body; some with neighbours; and one with the postman, who saw Wes Brackstone drive down Northampton Road at eight forty-five, like he did every morning.

Seb frowned. If Wes Brackstone had left the house at his usual time, then clearly Rosemary's statement was wrong. He turned several more pages and Rosemary's name came up again.

After consideration, Rosemary Fry realised that Wes did leave for work, but then returned home just before 9.30 in the morning. She explained her confusion was down to medication

Seb grimaced as he passed the notebook to Birdie. She read through it and made a soft grunting noise, no doubt at the redactions. She exchanged a glance with him, and he nodded.

'Can you explain why Rosemary Fry, the neighbour, changed her story? You mention her medication. What was she on that made her confused?' Birdie folded her arms, and stared directly at him. Not that it appeared to bother Dunbar.

'No idea.' Dunbar smirked.

'Also, there are several lines that have been crossed out, making it impossible to see what was there. Why did you do that?' Birdie continued.

'If you think my notes were bad, you should've seen Best's. He was a DI, but you'd think he was in nursery with the mess he made. I once saw him spill a pint over the whole book. The main thing is that we got the job done.'

'There's a lot to be said for old-school policing.' Seb forced a conciliatory tone. It seemed to work, and Dunbar laughed again.

'You're not wrong. As for the neighbour, if I remember right, at first she thought Wes hadn't left for work, but then remembered he had, and that he returned home shortly after.'

Birdie leant forward. 'I'm from Market Harborough, and I remember my mum telling me about all the lovely old trees that lined the streets. She said it was almost like a forest. So how would Rosemary even have been able to see the Brackstones' driveway?

Dunbar blinked, as if she'd asked him a ridiculous question. 'If your parents thought it was a forest, you might not want to go hiking with them. Trust me, I was there, and she could clearly see the driveway from her living-room window. More importantly, the jury agreed with us.'

'Of course,' Seb placated, before changing the topic. 'I'm curious about Wes Brackstone. I couldn't see any mention of him in your notebook. According to Rosemary's statement, he returned to the house before Helen's body had been discovered by her sister. Why wasn't he interviewed at the time?'

'You'll have to take that up with our dearly departed Detective Inspector Best,' Dunbar retorted, clearly happy to blame someone else for the numerous holes the case had already presented. 'He was the one who spoke to Brackstone while I got stuck with the postman.'

'Though you did interview him later.' Birdie held up the notebook in her hand. The ex-detective swallowed, and for the first time appeared rattled. 'This one's dated a week later. It looks like something else has been crossed out.'

She passed it over to Seb, clearly wanting him to commit it to memory. He calmly did so, and when he reached the part she'd mentioned, he read it out loud.

'"Interview with Wes Brackstone at suspect's house. He claims that he never went home that morning and that—"' Again several lines were crossed out so thoroughly it was impossible to read what was underneath it. The sentence picked up further along. '"Brackstone has no alibi and has refused to answer any of our questions."'

Seb looked over at Dunbar for an answer. The man simply shrugged.

'Like I said, Wes Brackstone didn't have an alibi. If he did, he would have used it in court. And that's why he was arrested a week after the murder.'

'Why did he first claim that he never went home? He must have had a reason for saying that. Why was it crossed out?' Birdie pushed, and Dunbar rubbed his brows, as if urging a memory to come forth.

'If I recall correctly, at first, he gave us the name of someone who could vouch for him. But when we said we'd contact them, Brackstone withdrew it. It's not that uncommon. DI Best told me to cross it out, since it was no longer relevant.'

'Why didn't you mention it in your notes?' Birdie asked.

'Because Best was handling it. He was convinced that Brackstone had simply panicked and made up a name.'

'And what about Helen's friend Carla? Did you speak to her?'

'Never heard of her. Was she at the scene?'

'Not as far as we're aware, but she was a long-time friend. She could have given valuable background information about Helen and Wes's marriage.'

'We had a dead body and a guilty husband. That's all the background we needed. Now, if that is all, I need to get ready. I'm playing golf this afternoon.'

Dunbar was clearly not going to give them anything further for the time being.

Seb stood up, closely followed by Birdie. They thanked Dunbar for his time and returned to the car. It wasn't until Seb had pulled away from the bungalow that Birdie let out an exasperated sigh.

'Twiggy clearly wasn't exaggerating. Dunbar seemed more than happy to blame everything on his DI. Still, I'm surprised he even spoke to us. And as for showing us his notebooks, that was a result. Especially considering such shoddy work. Sarge would have read me the Riot Act if I ever showed him anything like that.'

'I've met Dunbar's type before – smug and convinced that they're one step ahead of everyone else. It probably amused him to watch us trying to work it all out. I doubt he considered refusing us access to his notes because he believes he's foolproof.'

Seb slowed down as a tractor pulled in front of them on the narrow road. On each side of them, the green fields were flanked by low hedges and overhanging trees that helped shade the road. Finally, the lumbering farm vehicle turned off and Seb increased his speed.

'His mistake. And it's a doozy. Because he had no idea you can remember everything in his notebooks,' Birdie said, leaning back in her seat. 'I bet that would've stopped him looking so pleased with himself.'

'It's also possible that he's forgotten half of what he'd included.'

'I'm not buying that. He seemed to have all his wits about him. We certainly need to speak to Rosemary Fry as soon as possible. Did you hear back from Carla Brinkworth?'

Seb nodded. 'She returned my call last night and we're visiting her on Monday morning. Rosemary will have to wait until after then.'

'That's fine by me,' Birdie agreed. 'I've still got a couple of reports to finish on the Tipton and Allen cases. Then I can focus one hundred per cent on this case. Thank goodness it's Friday. I'm looking forward to slobbing out on the couch with a curry and a giant bar of chocolate this evening. What about you?'

'Are you asking whether I'll be "*slobbing out*"?' he asked, arching an eyebrow.

'You never know,' Birdie retorted. 'After all, when I first met you, you wore suits every day of the week, and now you not only wear jeans, but there isn't a crease ironed down the centre of them. It's a quick hop, skip and jump to full slob mode, and then my work here will be done.'

'I wait with bated breath.' Seb grinned, knowing that as close as he'd ever get to what Birdie called 'slobbing' was sitting on the couch with Elsa watching a rugby match. 'But in answer to your question, I'm visiting my parents.'

'Is Keira going with you? She's only just come back.'

'No. I'll head down after lunch on Saturday and should be back by Sunday evening. What about you? Cricket?'

Birdie nodded. 'It should be a good game, and since Keira will be here on her own, I'll ask if she wants to come and watch. Then we're off to the pub and dancing. Should be a good night. Hence why I need to conserve my energy this evening.'

Seb had yet to see his business partner run out of energy, but merely nodded his head. 'Wise, indeed. We should make the most of our downtime, because I suspect next week's going to be busy.'

SEVEN

Monday, 21 July

'I'm going about this house hunting business all wrong,' Birdie said on Monday morning as they walked through the reception area of Sunlight Mews Retirement Village. The new carpet and tasteful wallpaper were a far cry from the concrete stairwell of the prospective apartment she'd visited last week. Sun flooded through the long windows, which no doubt gave the place its name, and there was a main dining area with a choice of cafés, along with a hair salon, and several other shops. 'This place would suit me very well.'

'You might be a little young,' Seb reminded her as they continued through the main building and out into a grassy courtyard where Carla's flat was located. 'How was your weekend? Keira texted to say you won the match. Did you dance the night away?'

'Of course. It was Annie's birthday, so it would have been rude not to. It was a great night,' Birdie said, not bothering to add that she'd stayed in bed until the middle of the afternoon yesterday, trying to recover from her hangover.

It was totally worth it, though. Birdie couldn't remember the last time she'd gone out for a big night. Or when she'd had more fun. Most of the team had been there, and she'd bumped into a couple of old school friends as well. Not to mention Annie's cousin, Melinda – who had recently moved into the area and didn't know anyone – had joined them. Yes... it was a fun night.

'Glad to hear it. My parents send their love.'

Birdie dragged her thoughts back to the current conversation and burst out laughing. 'Seriously? Your dad said that? Did he blow me some kisses as well?'

'He's very sentimental once you get to know him,' Seb assured her, though his eyes were glinting.

Although she was no longer intimidated by Seb's aristocratic family, she doubted Viscount Worthington would say anything of the sort. But Seb's mum wasn't nearly as high and mighty as Birdie had once thought she'd be.

'I'm sure he is,' she agreed with a grin. 'I take it your visit went well?'

'Very,' he said, as they reached a row of bungalows. Number seven had a red front door that was surrounded by pots of pale pink flowers and a doormat with a picture of a hedgehog wearing a pair of spotted trousers. Clearly, Helen's old friend had a sense of humour.

They still didn't know much about her, other than she was eighty-one years old and appeared to be in good health. Seb pressed the bell and stepped back as they waited for the door to open. The elderly woman who opened the door had a round face and dark eyes. Her grey hair was cut short and curled around her ears.

'Hello, dears. You must be Sebastian. I'm Carla. Come in, come in.'

Carla led them through the small, self-contained unit into a tiny sitting room that looked out to a private garden. It was decorated in light colours and seemed very clean. A tea tray was already sitting on the low coffee table, along with several slices of cake and a plate of biscuits. It was clear the old woman had gone to some trouble, and Birdie wondered if it was because she didn't receive many visitors.

'Thank you for agreeing to see us,' Seb said. 'This is my partner, Birdie.'

'What an enchanting name.' Carla beamed and waved her arm in the direction of the small sofa. They both agreed to a cup of tea, and the older woman busied herself pouring before finally settling back into her own chair. 'So, how can I help? You mentioned Helen Brackstone on the phone.'

'That's right. How well did you know her?' Seb asked as Birdie took a bite of the clearly homemade cake, judging by its slightly lopsided shape. Yet another reason to live there if everyone baked as well as Carla.

'Very well. I first met her when I was at school. We lived a few doors down and her parents often hired me to babysit. She was probably only six at the time. Such a sweet, caring girl. We stayed friends as she grew older. There was ten years' difference between us, you see. There she is, over there.'

Birdie finished her mouthful of cake and turned towards the sideboard that was covered with a collection of silver-framed photographs.

'Would you mind if I took a look?'

'Of course not, dear.' Carla's eyes brightened. 'There are several from when she was younger, and some of Daryl, of course. They were like two peas in a pod. There's also one from her wedding.'

Birdie placed her plate on the table and crossed the room, followed by Seb. The first frame was of Helen wearing a black graduation gown, her smile wide as she threw her mortarboard up in the air. She must have been around twenty, and her brown hair was shoulder length. Her eyes were bright with joy.

It was a far cry from the photograph that most of the newspapers had used at the time, which had been of a scared-looking woman who appeared to be worried about something in the distance. Had they chosen it to make her look like a victim of domestic violence? Even though it was far from the truth.

'You're right. She does look like Daryl,' Seb said.

'Poor Daryl. She hated it when people asked if they were sisters. But I suspect she'd give anything for it to happen now.'

'It must have been difficult.'

Birdie picked up a second frame. It was of Helen and Wes outside the Market Harborough registry office. Helen was wearing a blue silk suit and tiny pillbox hat. She was smiling and staring up at Wes, who was dressed in a black suit and white shirt. He was smiling too.

'Is this from their wedding?' she asked Carla.

'Yes. It was a very small affair. But that's all they wanted.'

Again, this photo was a far cry from those in the newspapers. They'd only shown Wes with dishevelled hair and a pinched, angry mouth. It was nothing like the man in this photograph, who looked down at his new wife with pride and love. A lump formed in Birdie's throat at what a waste it was. At how different things might have been for them.

Stop it. She chided herself. Her job wasn't to feel sorry for the two people in the photograph. It was to get justice for them.

'Did Helen ever talk about TEC with you?' Birdie asked as she returned to her seat.

A shadow fell across Carla's face, and she put down her teacup, the saucer rattling. 'Yes. Helen was firm in her beliefs and very committed to that group.'

'How did she become involved with them?'

'It was while she was at university. She'd talk about them when she was home on her holidays and, at first, I wasn't too worried because her involvement only stretched as far as going to the occasional rally. But in her final year, she threw herself into the group. I never understood why it was so important to her.'

Seb frowned. 'Did she explain the group's aims and objectives? We haven't found much information online, and they've since disbanded.'

'That's one of the reasons I was worried about her involvement. In the pamphlets they used to hand out, they were very vague regarding what they were doing and who they were. Helen wouldn't name the other members, as if it was some sort of secret. From what I could gather, they focused on exposing corruption in big businesses and politics.'

A shiver of unease ran through Birdie. Helen being secretive about the organisation to her closest friend didn't bode well for what was really going on.

'Did Helen ever talk specifics about who they were targeting?' Birdie asked.

'No, I'm afraid not. It's not like now when everyone wears their beliefs on a T-shirt. Back then, she was always trying to keep everything private and separate.'

'Did you ever express any concerns about it?'

'Oh, yes. I told her that she was playing with fire. Men like that – and it was mainly men back then who were in positions of power – were only out for themselves. But she wasn't concerned. She said that's why she was in the collective. Because they wouldn't let anything happen to their members. She believed there was safety in numbers and that's why their anonymity was so important.'

Birdie rubbed her brow, not liking the growing picture she was getting. Despite how small they seemed to be, it appeared that TEC were not only passionate, but also naïve. Had someone come along and tried to eliminate them?

'Can you remember the last time you saw Helen?' Seb asked.

'I can. She worked for a charity in town, and I often

collected cans of food from my own workplace for them. I'd wait until I had several boxes and would take them over. On this particular day, Helen was thrilled to receive them, and we had lunch together. It was two weeks before...' Carla broke off, tears in her eyes, which she wiped away with a white hanky she'd produced from her sleeve.

'We know how hard this must be for you, and appreciate you talking to us,' Seb said. 'When you saw Helen that day, how did she seem? Did she mention anything specific about TEC?'

Carla closed her eyes, as if taking herself back to that moment in time. The pain in her face lessened, and she smiled. 'She was well enough, though perhaps a little distracted. But that wasn't uncommon. Like I said, she was very firm in her beliefs and was always worried about the state of the world. And of course, she had a husband and daughter, so was busy running the family home. But she didn't mention TEC specifically. I'm sure.'

'It must have been an awful shock when you heard what had happened,' Birdie said.

'Yes. At first I didn't believe it. You read about things like that in the paper and somehow think it can only happen to other people. Strangers. But to see Helen's name in the headlines and to read about how she died... It was terrible.'

'When the police arrested Wes, were you surprised? Did you believe he was responsible?' Birdie asked.

The question seemed to startle Carla, and her eyes widened. She picked up her handkerchief and rolled it between her fingers.

'Well... yes. Because they were a loving couple. I'm sure they had their problems, like most couples but murder... I couldn't believe it. But the police said they had evidence to prove it. And then he was found guilty at the trial.' Her hand fluttered in her lap, and she let out a worried moan. 'Are you saying that Wes didn't kill her? I know Daryl always believed her father was innocent... but I thought that was out of loyalty. Oh, dear.'

Birdie sucked in a breath. They needed to be careful not to cause the old woman further pain. Or make her feel guilty that possibly an innocent man had died in prison.

'That's what Daryl's hired us to discover,' Seb replied, stepping in. 'It's our job to consider all angles, so please don't distress yourself. It was up to the police to investigate at the time and there's nothing anyone else could have done.'

Some of the worry in Carla's eyes faded and she settled back into her chair. Birdie gave her partner an approving nod; his words appeared to have gone a long way in reassuring the woman.

'I should have realised. Poor Daryl. It's like a shadow's been following her around since it happened. I don't think she ever really recovered. That's why I try and stay in touch with her as best I can. To let her know she isn't completely alone.'

'That's very kind of you,' Seb agreed. 'We spoke to one of the detectives who worked on the case, and he said they didn't ever contact you. Were you surprised?'

'No, not really. I wasn't there at the time and wouldn't have been able to help them.'

'What can you tell us about Wes Brackstone? How well did you know him?'

'I wouldn't say I knew him well because I mainly spent time with Helen and Daryl. But I saw him plenty of times over the years at the house, and the wedding.'

'Would you say he was an angry man?'

Carla's mouth turned into a thoughtful line. 'Not angry... no. But Helen told me he didn't like her involvement with TEC and he'd sometimes moan about her job because it took up so much of her time. She always did have a habit of throwing herself into something if she believed in it. I think he wanted her to stay at home and look after Daryl.'

'Did the arguments ever get physical?' Birdie asked.

'Goodness me, no. Absolutely not. Wes loved Helen. Oh, dear. I should have gone to the police at the time and explained all this.' Carla's face paled she was clearly distressed.

'Please don't blame yourself. Do you think Helen feared him?' Birdie pressed.

'Again... no. They were the epitome of the phrase "opposites attract" but that made their relationship even stronger, from what I could see. Wes was happy with his little part of the world, whereas Helen always wanted to help those who couldn't help themselves. She wanted to make sure that Daryl and future generations were in safe hands.' An alarm clock rang from over by the sideboard, and Carla's shoulders stiffened. 'That's telling me it's time to take my tablets.'

Birdie placed her cup and saucer on the tray and gathered up Seb's and Carla's. 'We won't keep you any longer. But let me take these into the kitchen for you and wash up. Thank you for taking the time to speak to us.'

'Would you like me to fetch your tablets and some water?' Seb asked.

The elderly woman shook her head and slowly got to her feet. 'That's kind of you to offer, but no thanks. The carers will scold me if they think I'm not getting up from my chair enough. They like me to walk around when I can. I do hope I've been some help.'

'Yes, you have. If you think of anything else that might help, please call. You have my number,' Seb said.

Birdie moved to the neat kitchen, her mind spinning as she washed up. Seb dried beside her in silence as they processed the information Carla had given them.

Afterwards, they said their goodbyes and stepped out into the crisp air.

'I can't believe how everything was hung on Wes being a wife beater, and yet it's obvious he was in love with his wife and had no intention of harming her,' Birdie said, not even attempting to hide her frustration with the police.

'I agree,' Seb added.

Although it was The Equality Collective that had truly piqued Birdie's interest. A nagging thought tugged at her mind that there was more to this group than met the eye and she couldn't shake the sense they were standing on the edge of something much bigger. A mystery that was only just beginning to unfold.

EIGHT

Monday, 21 July

'I suggest we investigate TEC for a list of members and to discover what they were working on around the time of Helen's death in 1989,' Seb said as they made their way back to the car after interviewing Carla Brinkworth. 'We also need to know the depth of her involvement. It's entirely possible that all she did was attend meetings, leaving others to participate in more radical protests. If Carla's correct in her view that Helen's priority was Daryl and Wes, it stands to reason she might not have been too involved, for fear of repercussions should she have been arrested.'

'Yeah... I get what you're saying, but remember that Daryl told us her mum was often out every night. That seems pretty involved to me. Sarge said that, at the time, they'd pop up all over the place if there was a cause they believed in,' Birdie said, drumming her fingers impatiently on the side of Seb's car.

'We should contact Daryl now we know a little more.' Seb unlocked the car and they both climbed in. 'Although she couldn't remember much,' he continued, 'it might be because we didn't ask the right questions. Try her now.'

Birdie nodded in agreement and retrieved her phone, putting it on speaker so Seb could hear.

Their client answered on the third ring.

'Hi, Daryl,' Birdie said. She gave their client a quick recap on their conversation with Carla, and their visit to see Dunbar on Friday. 'We want to find out what TEC was involved in during the months leading up to your mother's death. If there's *anything* you can recall that might prove the depth of your mum's involvement with the group, it would be a big help.'

Daryl sighed. 'I'm sorry, but like I said, all I remember was that she went to meetings at night. There isn't...' There was a pause at the other end of the phone and then a small gasp. 'Of course. I totally forgot. There are several boxes in the loft that belonged to my parents. Aunt Kerry stored them after we moved back in.'

'Do you know what's in them?' Birdie asked, glancing at Seb, excitement in her eyes.

'No,' Daryl replied, sounding sheepish. 'At the time, I couldn't bear to even look at the outside of them. And then I forgot they were there... I'm very sorry.'

'No need to apologise. It's totally understandable that you didn't want to delve into the boxes. But how would you feel about going through them now?' Birdie asked, glancing at Seb and giving a thumbs up.

'I'm ready to do whatever it takes to discover the truth. I'll do it right now and let you know what I find.'

'Thanks so much. I'm sure it will help a lot.'

The rest of the journey they spent in relative silence and as Seb pulled up outside the front of Rendall Hall, Keira was in the garden with Elsa and glanced up at the sound of their tyres on the gravel. They both headed over as Seb and Birdie clambered out the car, Elsa's tail wagging furiously as she nudged Seb's leg in greeting.

'So? How did it go?' Keira asked.

'Really good,' Birdie said with a smile. 'Your dad and I reckon there is something in The Equality Collective, so we need to find out everything we can. Their members, what they were protesting about, and the depth of Helen's involvement.'

'I'm on it,' Keira said, hurrying back into the house.

Birdie and Seb followed at a more leisurely pace as they discussed the case. But once they reached the office, they all got to work.

After several hours, Seb rolled his shoulders and stood up, pleased with his discovery. Even with an ergonomic chair, his height made it difficult to remain seated for too long. Birdie had told him to buy a standing desk, but he enjoyed working at the antique desk, which was far more suited to the room they were in.

Keira was seated in the reading chair and Birdie hunched over her keyboard at her own desk, foot tapping against the floor as she worked. It had taken a while, but he was now used to her fidgeting and could block it out most of the time. Especially because it was often a sign that her research was progressing well. As if on cue, she glanced up at him, her eyes gleaming against her pale skin and smattering of freckles.

He knew that look.

'Good news?'

'Yeah, and it looks like you've found something, as well. I'll tell you mine if you tell me yours,' Birdie teased.

Keira let out a groan from the corner. 'You two are ridiculous. You know that, right?'

'If you say so.' Seb bit back his amusement. He'd noticed that the more comfortable Keira became with them both, the happier she was to tell them how embarrassing they were.

Several of his friends had assured him that it was a rite of passage. However, Birdie's red curls seemed to frizz in response.

'Ridiculous? We're not the ones who changed clothes five times before going to the pub last Tuesday night. *Tuesday,*' Birdie repeated, as if it was somehow important.

Keira's mouth dropped open, but then she returned Birdie's wink.

Clearly, it meant something, but Seb had no idea what that might be. And he wasn't going to ask because he didn't want Keira to think of him as an interfering father. At her age she needed space.

'Fair call.' Keira held up her hands in defeat.

Seb headed over to Birdie's desk. 'Now, let's hear what you've unearthed.'

'The Equality Collective was set up in 1971 at Leicester University, which is where Helen studied sociology. It was part of a New Left movement that didn't trust the government to fix the "miserable state of the country" – their words, not mine,' Birdie clarified. 'While some groups protested the Vietnam War and nuclear power, TEC were focused on marginalised communities, including ethnic minorities, women, and the economically disadvantaged. They believed that they'd inherited a world that allowed big business and politicians to take advantage of these groups.'

'Yes,' Seb said. 'There was a huge mistrust of the government at the time. There were strikes, the Troubles in Ireland, and more than a million people unemployed. Numerous groups appeared who preferred to take direct, radical action instead of non-violent protests.'

Keira's eyes were wide. 'Sounds like the internet but in real life. Do you know how deep Helen's involvement was?'

'As it happens, I do.' Birdie broke out in a wide smile. 'I found the minutes of the initial meeting, and Helen was listed as attending. That means she was involved, right from the start. Other people at the initial meeting were' – Birdie checked her screen – 'Mark Grant, Lily Chen, Russell McAllister and Gail O'Reilly. I haven't yet had a chance to research into them.'

At the mention of Mark Grant, Seb grimaced. 'I've been reading old newspaper articles that mention TEC,' he said. 'They were often mentioned, but usually as a group, rather than being individually named. We know that Helen was never arrested – because if she had been, it would have come up in the case, or Twiggy would have found it when he did the search for you. But I did find one article mentioning Mark Grant. I'll forward it to you.' Seb returned to his desk and sent over the article.

'And?' Birdie leant forward. 'Don't keep us in suspense.'

'Sorry. You can both read it in full when you receive it, but to summarise, a government minister visited Leicester to open a building. TEC was there and Mark Grant threw red paint over the minister. He was arrested and, according to another article I read, given community service.'

'When I spoke to Sarge, he didn't remember there being any arrests,' Birdie said, frowning. 'Then again, this happened in Leicester and not Market Harborough, so maybe he didn't know about it.'

'This proves they were a radical group,' Seb continued. 'It's also possible that Helen was there when Grant was arrested. That needs checking.'

'On it,' Keira announced as her fingers glided across the keyboard of her laptop.

Seb returned to scanning through all the articles reporting on TEC, of which there were many. But there were no more arrests, and while he was sifting through some of the student newspapers of the time, Keira let out a squeal. She jumped up from the chair and walked over to the whiteboard they used while working on a case. Even though she shared his HSAM, she preferred using the board to help visualise all possible components.

'Mark Grant was a politics student who graduated in 1973 and went on to become a journalist. But he died fifteen years ago,' Keira said as she wrote it up. She also added some pertinent details about TEC.

'Before you sit down, I've got more details for you to add,' Birdie said. 'Lily Chen graduated the same year and while I can't find out where she worked, she did move to Australia. Russell McAllister also became a journalist, but no longer works for the publication listed. I haven't yet managed to find where he lives. That leaves Gail O'Reilly.'

Seb tapped her name into the computer. 'There's a Gail O'Reilly in West Bridgford, Nottingham. She appears to be the right age, and she attended university in Leicester. Since flying to Australia isn't quite in the budget, Gail's the best place to start.'

'I'll look for her address,' Keira said.

Seb's phone buzzed. He checked the screen. 'It's Daryl.'

'Sebastian, I hope I'm not disturbing you,' their client said as Seb answered. 'But I've been through the boxes and have found several things. I can bring them to you, if you like.'

He rubbed his jaw.

'We'd rather visit you, if we may.'

'Of course,' Daryl agreed. 'I have an errand to run but will be back by one. Does that suit? The street parking is shocking, so make sure you park on my driveway.'

'Will do. Thanks.' He finished the call and Birdie joined him at his desk.

'What is it?' Birdie asked, rubbing her hands together.

'She's found something in the boxes. I don't know what but it's clearly something relevant. It will also be useful to see the property to ascertain how easy or difficult it would have been to gain access.'

'I'd like to see the view Rosemary Fry had of the driveway where she allegedly saw Wes's car parked.' Birdie's stomach rumbled. 'But tell me we've got time to eat first.'

'We're not expected until one, so there's plenty of time.'

'Good, because I'm starving too.' Keira shut her laptop and headed for the door. 'While you and Birdie are out, I'll continue looking for Gail O'Reilly's address. I'll let you know when I find it.'

'Sounds like a plan.' Birdie followed Keira out to the kitchen, leaving Seb alone.

He'd make a sandwich in a minute, but first he wanted to collect his thoughts to make sure they hadn't missed anything before they visited the place where Helen had been murdered.

NINE

Monday, 21 July

'This is the posh part of the road in case you can't tell,' Birdie informed Seb as she got out of the car and joined him at the front door of Daryl's home in Northampton Road.

It was a large three-storey red-brick semi-detached house with mock Tudor detail above the second-storey bay window. Seb had to agree that the house was a fine example of Edwardian architecture; a datestone had been set into the archway above the small entrance, with the year 1905 carved into the limestone. The front door had several stained-glass panels set into it, through which Seb observed the outline of someone walking towards it, before he could press the bell.

Moments later, the door opened and Daryl appeared.

'I was looking out of the window and saw you arrive,' she explained while welcoming them inside. The hallway was bright and cheery, with high ceilings and picture rails running along each wall. She gestured them into the front reception room, which looked out onto the street. 'Would you like a drink?'

'No thanks,' Birdie said. 'We've just had lunch. If you don't mind, before we go through the boxes, can we look around? It will help us build a picture of what occurred.'

Daryl swallowed and her fingers knotted together.

'If it's easier, we can look on our own,' Seb said. 'While there's no police report available, Jeff Dunbar did show us his notebook, so we have a good idea of the events and how they unfolded.'

Relief flooded Daryl's face. 'Okay. If you're happy to do that. I know it sounds daft because it all happened so long ago and I've lived here all this time... But now we're actually—'

'It's no problem. You don't need to explain,' Birdie interrupted, smiling kindly at the woman.

'Thanks. I'll wait in here for you. It, uh, took place in the kitchen, which is down the hall. The key to the garden is in the back door. The kitchen's been renovated since it happened, but I didn't change the footprint, so it's all as it was at the time.'

'That's good to know,' Birdie said.

They left Daryl alone and made their way down the long hallway into a dining room that led through to the large, square kitchen.

Daryl had clearly resisted the urge to turn it into an open-plan space when she renovated, and the original wall was still there, including the cavity where a fireplace had once been, although it now contained a collection of cookbooks. The dining room was sparse, mainly taken up with a long farmhouse table and six chairs.

'This was where she was found,' Birdie said, walking to the head of the table before peering at the sash windows on the exterior wall. They were wide and helped fill the room with light. 'Assuming that it wasn't Wes who murdered Helen, how did the person get into the house?'

'She might have let them in through the front door if the person was known to her,' Seb replied.

'And if it was a stranger, they could've climbed in through one of these windows. Or come in through the back door.'

'Either way, they'd have to get into the back garden first. Which would depend on whether the entry gate was locked or not,' Seb reasoned.

'True. But they could have accessed it via the neighbour's.' Birdie pointed to the wooden fence separating the two properties.

'Irrespective of whether it was a stranger, or someone Helen knew, they managed to get inside the house. Then what occurred to ensure she drank the poison? She would have smelt it, so giving her a drink wouldn't have worked because she would have refused. That leaves force, but there was no suggestion in Dunbar's notes that the scene suggested a struggle.'

Seb frowned and walked around the table, trying to imagine someone standing next to Helen.

Birdie's face darkened, and she clenched her fists. 'It's so annoying that we don't have a pathology report. If we did we'd know if there was bruising or other signs of trauma around her mouth and neck.'

'There's no point in letting that frustrate you, because we can't do anything about it. Let's take a look in the garden,' Seb suggested.

They walked through the kitchen and he unlocked the back door, putting the keys in his pocket, and stepped outside. Despite the changes, it appeared that the original back door and frame had been left intact.

The long, narrow garden was south-west facing, and Seb inspected the internal dividing fence. It didn't look to have been replaced in years, and it wouldn't have been difficult for someone to climb over. On the other hand, entering from the back was far more tricky. A high brick wall, with a locked gate, separated the property from the open fields behind the house. Using one of the keys on the keyring from the back door, Seb opened the gate and stepped out onto a path. There was a narrow entry beside the wall that led to the front of the house, and while there was another locked wrought-iron gate to get through, there was still a possibility that the killer could have gained access.

Seb headed back into the garden to where Birdie had crouched down and was inspecting the back-door frame. 'Look at this,' she said, after noticing him standing beside her.

She pointed to an area where the barrel was embedded into the wood and he bent down to study it. There were several light gouges along the wood, and while they'd been painted over, it was clear to see the grooves. There were matching ones on the side of the door. He frowned. They'd both visited enough crime scenes over the years to recognise when a door had been levered open. He ran his finger along the paint, though it was hard to tell how long the dents had been there.

'Is everything okay?' Daryl appeared at the doorway.

'We're not sure,' Birdie admitted. 'Have you ever had a break-in?'

'No, never,' Daryl answered immediately. 'My parents were extremely security conscious and kept the doors and ground-floor windows locked, even when we were home. I've inherited that trait. My father always said that we shouldn't make it easy for opportunists.'

Seb pointed to the indents on the door frame. 'Birdie discovered these. They look like the result of someone trying to gain entry to the property. Do you recall when this happened?'

'No. I remember seeing them when I painted, but didn't think anything of it. With an old house like this, there are always a few bumpy, crooked things.' Colour drained from her face. 'Do you think someone forced their way into the house the day my mother was killed?'

'It's possible, but it's a large leap to make at this stage. Although, there certainly appears to have been an attempted break-in at some stage. Whether or not they were successful, we don't yet know. Thank you for allowing us to look around. Are you ready to discuss the boxes' contents?'

'Yes, of course.' Daryl swallowed, still visibly flustered by their comments.

They followed her through the kitchen, down the hallway and into the front room, which was flooded with sunshine. What appeared to be original wooden floors gave it a warm feeling. The low coffee table was covered in old manilla folders and to one side were several boxes, liberally coated with dust, together with a pile of documents.

'I haven't had a chance to go through everything, but the files on the table all have my mother's handwriting on the front, so I thought you could start with them while I continue looking through the other boxes. Some things are old household accounts and documents, so I'm trying to separate them all out.'

'Thanks. We'd like to go through any financial records, too. That's Seb's speciality, and if there is anything unusual to be gleaned from them, he'll be the one to find it,' Birdie said.

'Of course. Whatever you think will help.' Daryl dropped down onto the floor and lifted the lid on one of the boxes. Birdie joined Daryl on the floor, while Seb started going through the tower of folders.

He quickly discovered that Helen was exceptionally well organised. Clipped together were pages of handwritten notes as well as a yellowing article that had been cut out from a newspaper. There was also a collection of photocopied pages from a planning-permission application.

Several applications had been submitted to the Leicester City Council by a development company who wanted to build an office block in an area that was currently zoned as residential. He turned his attention back to the newspaper article.

Save Our Estate.

Despite the name Riddle Park, residents are not laughing at the proposed plans to bulldoze their homes to make way for a new office development. First built just after the Second World War, Riddle Park was once a safe place to live, but over the last twenty years, it has fallen into disrepair and been given the dubious honour of being one of England's worst examples of social housing. But according to Moira Reynolds, who moved to the estate in 1971, it was like winning the pools after years of living in an flat full of mould. And while she agrees that there has been some bad press, most of the residents are law-abiding citizens. She added that the downfall was because of the lack of work in the area, which had forced so many people into crime.

'Pulling it down won't fix the problem,' Moira said at a community meeting, where over fifty residents gathered to protest the proposed plans. 'This is our home and we're not going anywhere.' It was a sentiment echoed by others in attendance.

He finished reading and then passed the article to Birdie.

'It looks like Helen was gathering information about a proposed set of office blocks being built on a housing estate called Riddle Park. It's in Leicester. Are you familiar with it?'

Birdie put down the folder she was studying and joined him on the sofa. 'Riddle Park estate? Yes, I've heard of it and as far as I know it was knocked down to make way for the offices that the article mentions. The planning must have gone ahead.' She pulled out her phone and did a quick search. 'Yes, it all went through in the early nineties. The new development was called Camberton Towers. More offices have gone up since then, but that was the first one.'

'The newspaper article is from March 1989, two months before Helen's death,' Seb said. 'There's a good chance this was what she was working on at the time. Daryl, did you ever hear your mother mention Riddle Park or construction in Leicester?'

'No. But that doesn't mean she didn't. She went to university there, and would often talk about it... I remember sometimes tuning her out.' Regret marred her features, and it was clear it continued to cause her pain.

Seb thought of the occasional eye roll that Keira gave him when she thought he was being too old-fashioned. Then remembered his own lack of interest in his parents when he was a teenager. It was nothing out of the ordinary.

'It doesn't matter,' Birdie quickly assured their client, obviously also picking up on Daryl's distress. 'It seems like your mother made a lot of notes. What else is in that file, Seb? Does it say who built the development?'

'Yes. A company called Fullerton Construction.' He handed over some of the papers so she could also read through them. It would speed up the search.

Seb returned to Helen's meticulous notes. She'd spoken to several journalists, including the one who had written the article about the residents being unhappy. Helen had also listed the names of several other people who worked for the local government.

'Look at this.' Birdie pushed back an errant curl and handed over some sheets of paper. 'If I'm reading this correctly, Helen suspected Fullerton Construction of paying off people to ensure to their applications went through and they got planning permission.'

Seb scanned the list. It was simply headed *Fullerton*, and underneath was a list of four amounts of money ranging from eight hundred and fifty pounds to five thousand pounds. However, there were no account details or any names. Just the initial *MB* next to each amount.

'There isn't enough information to prove these were bribes.'

'I agree. And who's MB? Were they the person receiving

the bribes, or could they be the person informing Helen about it? Either way, it's worth investigating.'

'I have my mum's old address book. I'll check if there's anyone with those initials.' Daryl stood up and crossed the room.

Seb's phone buzzed with a text message.

> Success. Gail O'Reilly lives at 10 Chester Crescent, West Bridgford, Nottingham. No phone number though.

He sent back a quick reply and looked over to where Birdie was staring at him expectantly.

'Keira's discovered where Gail lives,' he explained.

Birdie broke into a broad smile. 'She never ceases to impress me with her research skills... Daryl, is there anyone in the address book with those initials?'

'No. Sorry. My mother was very organised, and I've checked under *M* and *B*. Who's Gail?'

'A TEC member. She lives about an hour away and we've now got her address,' Birdie explained. 'We're hoping she can give us more information on TEC and Helen's involvement. Though having these files is a huge help. May we take the rest of the boxes with us? We can go through them properly once we're back at the office.'

'Of course. Like I said, I'm happy for you to do whatever it takes.' Daryl began to pack away. 'Thank you both. I'm now even more convinced that things were overlooked in the original investigation.'

'It's too early for us to speculate, but we'll do our best to get to the truth,' Seb assured her, but conscious that they shouldn't give their client false hope.

After loading the boxes into the boot of the car, Seb glanced across the busy street at the matching set of semi-detached houses. Directly opposite was number eighteen.

Rosemary Fry's house.

'I know that look,' Birdie said, following his gaze. She let out a breath. 'Is that where the neighbour who changed her testimony lived?'

'It is,' Seb confirmed as a truck lumbered past them, temporarily breaking the view. 'Dunbar wrote down the address in his notebook.'

'Yes, and conveniently forgot to mention it was across the road and not next door. This is one of the busier arterial roads and added to the fact that there are trees on both sides of the road, it makes it even harder to trust the statement. I wonder if Rosemary Fry still lives there?' Birdie said. 'There's one way to find out.' She moved to the edge of the kerb, standing beside the road waiting for a break in the traffic. Except it was nose to tail as far as the eye could see.

Finally, she was able to dart across, and Seb observed her walking up to the door and knocking. After several minutes with no answer, she gave up and joined him in the car.

'So much for that idea,' Birdie said, tutting.

'We'll follow up with her tomorrow,' Seb said as he keyed Gail O'Reilly's address into the car's satnav.

Birdie gave a reluctant sigh. 'I know. But patience never was my strong suit.' She retrieved her phone from her bag and scrolled through her messages before turning to him. 'I'll give Keira a call and ask her to check Fullerton Construction and the names of the local government officers at the time. With a bit of luck she might turn up someone with the initials *MB*.'

Seb started the engine. 'If Gail isn't home, we might have time to come back via Leicester and have a look for ourselves, since it's on the way.'

Birdie dipped her head in agreement before making the call as Seb waited for another rare gap in the traffic and headed in the direction of the M1 and towards West Bridgford.

TEN

Monday, 21 July

Gail O'Reilly lived in a modest semi-detached house, buried deep in a cul-de-sac on an estate full of identical homes.

'No wonder the front doors are painted different colours. Otherwise, how could you tell them apart?' Birdie muttered as they got out of the car.

'If only someone thought to give them different numbers,' Seb retorted, quirking an eyebrow.

'Like that idea's going to catch on,' she quipped with a grin as they walked up the path to number ten.

With the start of the school holidays, neighbourhood children were dotted up and down the street, making the most of the July sunshine. A cacophony of laughter and high-pitched voices surrounded them. Some of the kids were standing chatting, others were with their bikes, and a few of them kicked around a football.

Seb pressed the doorbell, and it was answered by a woman in her seventies. She was petite with straight white hair that came down to her shoulders, and was wearing jeans and slippers. At the sight of them, her grey eyes clouded, and she gripped at the door frame with her spare hand.

'Can I help you?'

'We hope so,' Seb said softly. 'I'm Sebastian Clifford and this is Birdie. We're private investigators. Are you Gail O'Reilly?'

'That's correct,' Gail said, not relinquishing her grip. 'What's this about?'

'We've been hired to investigate the death of Helen Brackstone. We understand that you and Helen were members of The Equality Collective years ago, and we're hoping you could spare us a few minutes to answer some questions,' Seb said.

Her mouth twisted in surprise. 'Helen Brackstone? Now that's a name I haven't heard in a long while. Why are you looking into her death after all this time?'

'Daryl, her daughter, hired us. She's never accepted that her father was guilty,' Birdie explained.

Gail nodded in understanding. 'That poor girl. She was only fourteen at the time. Though, I suppose she's a grown woman now. I never met her in person, but have thought of her occasionally over the years. Please, come in. I'm not sure how useful I can be, but I'm happy to answer any questions you have.'

'We appreciate that. Thank you,' Seb said.

Not everyone was prepared to discuss a case when asked, and Seb and Birdie weren't able to insist. It was one of the main differences between his time in the police and working as a private investigator. But since opening the business, he and Birdie had found that the more open they were, the more likely it was that people would assist.

They followed her into the house and through to the small sitting room, which was filled with a sofa and two reclining chairs. Framed photographs of who Seb assumed were family covered the walls. The television in the corner was tuned to a news channel, but the sound was muted.

On one of the chairs was a bag of knitting, and Gail put it to one side and settled down, while Birdie took the other recliner, leaving Seb the sofa.

'When did you first meet Helen?' Birdie asked.

'At university. I was studying geography, but we were both involved in TEC and became friends. Back then, we wanted to save the world.' She let out a bitter laugh. 'Look how well we've done. Nothing has changed.'

'Are you still in touch with the other members?'

'No. Poor Mark died years ago, and I lost touch with Lily after she moved abroad. As for Russell... He was always a loose cannon, and we never knew where he was living or what he was up to. The last I heard, he was teaching English in Japan, but that was over twenty years ago.'

'We're trying to create a timeline of what Helen was working on at the time of her death. In her belongings, there's a folder of information involving a proposed development at Riddle Park in Leicester. What do you know about that?' Seb asked, leaning forward slightly.

'Helen could be like a truffle hound when something captured her attention, and Riddle Park was one of those,' Gail said, her eyes taking on a distant look as she traced patterns on her leg with her finger. 'We discussed the planning application at several of our meetings, but there were several other things on the agenda, and our focus was more on them. But Helen became obsessed and wouldn't let it go.'

'In what way?' Birdie wanted to know.

'Well, she was particularly concerned about what would happen to the residents if the estate was pulled down. At the time, the tabloids dubbed them all as "spongers" who were only interested in claiming state benefits and causing trouble. It wasn't true, of course, but when have people ever cared about the truth? Those sensational headlines were very damaging.'

'It would have made it easier for the developers to go ahead with their plans,' Seb agreed.

Gail's face darkened in agreement. 'Unfortunately, that playbook's still in use today. Demonise the enemy, then swoop in with a solution. Helen was frustrated that, apart from a couple of journalists, no one would take up the cause and listen to what the Riddle Park residents had to say.'

'We saw an article about a community meeting that took place,' Birdie mentioned.

'Like I said, Helen was persistent and managed to get a couple of journalists interested. But when she suggested there was something underhand going on between the developers and the local planning office – corruption – they backed off.'

'Did Helen have any proof of this?' Birdie furrowed her brows.

'She said she did, but didn't tell us what it was. Towards the end of her life, she started to become paranoid about who to trust.'

'In what way?' Seb asked.

'She received several phone calls telling her to stop digging, and one time when she arrived at a meeting, she was terrified. Because she was convinced she was being followed.'

'That's serious. Did she go to the police?' Birdie asked.

'No, she didn't. We should perhaps have encouraged her to, but you must understand how things were back then. Between us, we'd been threatened, sworn at, and physically removed from protests, so our trust in the police wasn't high. Also – although we could never prove anything – we believed there was a lot of corruption within the force.' Gail sank back into her chair, fatigue draining her face of colour.

'Am I right in assuming that Helen didn't back down despite feeling threatened?' Seb asked.

Gail finally gave a wry smile. 'Helen never backed down from anything. It's funny because you'd never have known that's what she was like if you looked at her. She dressed like a conservative housewife, but underneath, she was tenacious. It's what helped us get TEC off the ground. Without her, I doubt we would've done much more than rant about the state of the nation.'

'Did she ever mention where her information about Riddle Park came from?' Birdie asked.

'No. All she said was someone in Leicester's local government planning office was helping. We didn't push for further details – it was important to keep secret the names of people who helped our cause.'

'What about the initials *MB*?' Seb asked. 'Do they mean anything to you?'

Gail was silent as she considered it, obviously sifting through names in her mind, but in the end, she gave them an apologetic look.

'Sorry, I can't think of anyone with those initials. Like I said though, Helen would often go off on her own, and it wasn't unusual for her not to confide in us.'

'How did you and the other TEC members react when you heard about Helen's death?' Seb asked.

Again, a look of something crossed her face and she rubbed her eyes.

'We were all devastated, of course. Most of us had known her for twenty years, and while we'd all gone our separate ways compared to our student days, we still felt like a family. After Helen's death, we tried to keep TEC going, but it wasn't the same.'

'Considering what Helen had been working on, and the threats she mentioned, did you think her death was suspicious?' Seb asked, tilting his head slightly to one side.

'No, because I believed what the police told us about her

husband, Wes. None of us had ever met him, you see. Helen preferred to keep the two parts of her life separate. I guess we all did. I went to the funeral and saw her daughter, but didn't introduce myself. I didn't want to intrude.' Gail swallowed and fished for a handkerchief up her sleeve, which she used to wipe her eyes. 'I regret that now.'

'She might not have remembered even if you had because it was so overwhelming,' Birdie said. 'It would have been very hard for anyone to deal with, let alone a child.'

'It was,' Gail agreed, nodding. 'I might be overstepping the mark here, but if you think it's appropriate, please tell Daryl that I'd like to meet her.'

'That's a kind offer,' Seb acknowledged, careful not to make any promises.

The lines of fatigue reappeared on Gail's face, and it was clear she was finding the conversation tiring. Birdie shifted in her seat, indicating they should leave. He agreed, but had one more question.

'I'm curious. Did the police ever contact you about Helen's death?'

It seemed to catch Gail off guard, and her mouth dropped open slightly. 'No, they didn't. At the time, I didn't think anything of it because we had so little faith in them... but they should have, shouldn't they?'

'It's easy to be wise after the event,' Seb said as he stood. 'We won't take up any more of your time, but thank you. You've been a great help.'

'If you do think of anything else, please give us a call,' Birdie said as she extracted a business card from her phone case and left it on the coffee table.

Gail got to her feet and clutched Seb's arm, her grey eyes still troubled. 'I will. Please let me know what you find out because if she was killed by someone other than Wes, it could mean she was right about the corruption, and that she was silenced. It was everything we were trying to fight against. Oh, and her poor husband—' Her voice broke, and Seb patted her hand.

'If an innocent man went to jail, we'll do our best to prove it.'

'Yes,' Birdie agreed, her eyes flashing with determination.

Gail gave them both a grateful smile.

'You both remind me of Helen. She'd be pleased to know that members of TEC weren't the only ones who cared about the truth.'

They took their leave, but it wasn't until they'd driven away from the estate and joined the peak-hour traffic, all heading in the direction of the M1, that Seb finally spoke.

'It's ironic that they probably spent most of their time being told by society that they were too paranoid about conspiracies and corruptions, and yet when one of their members was murdered, they accepted it. Then again, because Helen kept her family life separate, they wouldn't have had enough reason to question Wes's arrest and sentencing.'

'A double-edged sword if ever there was one,' Birdie said. 'At least now we have a better idea of who Helen was. Determined but cautious. Judging by the files Daryl gave us, she wanted to cross her *T*s and dot her *I*s before taking anything back to the other members.'

'Someone was disturbed enough by her investigation to make threatening calls and follow her.' Seb gripped the steering wheel as they merged onto the motorway. It was almost five in the afternoon and the traffic was sluggish as they drove past the untamed trees that hid the villages and towns from the busy road.

'Exactly, yet Dunbar insisted there was no reason to investigate TEC. It makes me so angry.'

Birdie retrieved her phone and checked her messages. Out of the corner of his eye, Seb could see her frown.

'Something wrong?'

'No... I've had two calls from a number I don't recognise, but they didn't leave a message.'

Seb was about to comment when his own phone, which was connected to the car, began to ring, and Keira's name flashed up on the dashboard's display screen.

He answered the call. 'We're on our way back. Is everything okay?'

'You bet it is,' Keira's excited voice boomed out through the car speakers. 'You might want to pick up takeaway for us all on your way home because I've got news for you both.'

'Care to share?' Birdie asked, but Keira just laughed.

'Where's the fun in that? Besides, it's not like you can do anything until you're here. Be prepared for a late night. I'll fill you in when you're back.'

'Your daughter has a flair for melodrama,' Birdie complained, once the call had ended. Although she was grinning.

It was contagious, and Seb felt a stab of pride. Keira was so much more outgoing than he could ever remember being, and combined with her dedication and quick mind, she continued to amaze him.

'I can always catch you up tomorrow if you already have plans for the night?' he offered.

'Please... Do you really think I'm going to miss out on all the fun? Aside from what Keira wants to tell us, we still have the rest of Helen's files to look through. If only that truck would speed up, we could get there faster.'

Seb smiled at her impatience and waited until it was safe to overtake. They would be home soon enough.

ELEVEN

Monday, 21 July

'Okay, you've had your dumplings, now spill the beans on what you've found,' Birdie said after they'd eaten dinner and she was wiping down the worktop. She levelled her gaze at Keira, who was still fizzing with excitement. 'And you really need to work on your poker face, because your expression is practically shouting that you've discovered something big about the case.'

'Duly noted,' Keira said, mimicking Seb. He raised an eyebrow at her, and she giggled. 'Only joking, Dad. Anyway, I discovered a couple of things. Fullerton Construction went into receivership ten years after Helen died, and their managing director moved to Switzerland not long after. His name's Roger North.'

'Damn, that's over twenty-five years ago. Which means the company didn't exactly prosper, even if they were up to something dodgy.' Birdie frowned.

'It also means that crime doesn't pay,' Keira joined in. 'But wait, there's more. Drumroll please...' She tapped rhythmically on the worktop with her fingers. 'I've tracked down our mysterious "MB". Maurice Bryant was a planning officer for the council, and he was working there in 1989 when Helen first started looking into Fullerton's application to build the office block.'

Birdie's own eyes widened, and she let out a whistle. 'Nice work, Keira.'

'I know, right? And you said Gail confirmed that Helen had an informant at the council. I'll bet anything that Bryant was that person.'

'It's a possibility,' Seb agreed. He didn't want to dampen Keira's spirit, but he knew better than to jump to conclusions. 'It's also possible that he was bribed by Fullerton Construction. Either way, it means we now have something to work with. Birdie's right, it's very good work.'

'Thanks. You're right, though. He could easily be the villain and not the hero,' Keira said, letting out a long sigh. 'I haven't been able to find out anything else about him...'

'Look, you can't expect to solve all this in an afternoon,' Birdie said. 'We're here now to help. Fresh eyes and all that...'

'Fresh eyes and mad skills,' Keira retorted, making a bowing motion with her arms in Birdie's direction. Then she turned to Seb and patted his arm. 'And you have some *good* skills, too.'

'That's a relief.' Seb's lips twitched with amusement as he followed them back through to the office, enjoying their easy banter before they all returned to their computers.

At his own desk, happy to let Birdie continue with the research into Bryant, Seb opened one of the box files that they'd brought in from the car to start analysing Helen's financial records.

The room fell silent as they all became absorbed in their work. Seb separated the different bank statements into joint and individual, and focused on Helen's from 1988 to 1989. Most of her expenses didn't ring any alarm bells, apart from one: she'd made weekly payments into a bank account belonging to a

Gordon Black over a ten-month period, which stopped two weeks before her death. A quick internet search revealed nothing about this person and he picked up his phone, intending to call Daryl, when Birdie jumped up.

'I've got something.'

Seb swivelled to face her. 'Excellent. What is it?'

'The reason Keira couldn't find Maurice Bryant anywhere is because he died two months after Helen, on the fifteenth of July 1989. I found it in the obituary section of the *Mercury*.'

Keira let out a groan, pushing her hair back off her face. 'I'm such an idiot. Why didn't I think to check death notices?'

'Because it's all part of the learning curve, and next time you will,' Birdie said.

There was no hint of teasing in Seb's partner's voice, and Keira soaked it up. Birdie was an excellent teacher.

'What was the cause of death?' Seb asked.

'It doesn't say. The obit was one line and mentioned that he was thirty-five at the time of death.'

Thirty-five was young. Seb's skin prickled. Was Bryant a second victim?

'Was he married?' he asked. 'Is there a wife, children or family member we can talk to? Because it seems like too much of a coincidence that he died two months after Helen.'

'I couldn't agree more. He was married to Freda Bryant, who's still very much alive. She's in a care home in Lutterworth and because you have a knack of charming your way into those places, I thought you might like to contact them. I've texted you the number.'

'Not sure I would call it a *knack*,' Seb protested as he picked up his phone and retrieved the number. Although it was almost seven, he assumed that there would be a receptionist on duty. It was answered on the second ring, and he quickly made his introduction.

'How can I help you, Mr Clifford?'

'We're currently working on a case which we'd like to discuss with one of your residents. Freda Bryant. Would you be kind enough to ask her if she'd be prepared to talk to us?'

'If you'd like to hold on for a bit, I'll ask. Bingo's about to finish, so don't worry if you suddenly hear a lot of noise.' She laughed. 'I won't be long.' Seb waited for a couple of minutes until the woman returned. 'Hello? Are you still there?' she asked.

'Yes,' Seb said.

'Freda said she's happy to speak to you tomorrow after lunch, which is at twelve. She's such a sweetheart and rarely has any visitors.'

'Thank you, we'll be there at two. Enjoy the rest of your evening,' Seb said, as he ended the call.

'See... Charm oozes out of you when it comes to nursing homes.' Birdie smirked. 'Keira, you had better add that to his skill set.'

'It's in the vault.' Keira tapped her skull, then narrowed her eyes. 'You know something else, don't you, Dad?'

'Yes. Having gone through Helen's bank statements, I discovered a regular payment to a Gordon Black that I can't account for. I was about to call Daryl to see if she recognises the name.'

Birdie leant over to the pile of bank statements on his desk and let out a long whistle. 'You got through all of them already? I'd lose my mind trying to concentrate on all those numbers.'

'I enjoy the challenge of looking for anomalies,' Seb admitted as he picked up the phone.

Daryl answered his call immediately. 'Sebastian. Is everything okay?'

'Sorry about the late call. I've got you on speaker.'

'Hello, Daryl,' Birdie said.

'I've been going through your mother's personal bank statements and discovered payments made to a Gordon Black.

Do you know who he is and why she'd be paying him?' Seb asked.

'Gordon Black?' Daryl let out a sharp breath. 'Are you sure?'

'I take it you know him?' Birdie's shoulders straightened.

'Yes, but... I'm trying to work out why Mum would have given him any money. He was her cousin, but they weren't close. I only met him once when he came to visit. Dad was really unhappy when he turned up. From what I could gather, he was considered bad news.'

'Did he go to your mother's funeral? Or stay in touch with Kerry afterwards?' Seb asked.

'I don't remember seeing him at the funeral, and I've never heard from him. As for whether he stayed in contact with Kerry after Mum's death, I couldn't say. She certainly never mentioned it, but I do know that she had no time for him, either.'

'Why was he considered bad news?' Birdie asked.

There was a pause from the other end of the phone, as if Daryl was trying to dredge up a memory, but then she let out a soft sigh. 'I can't remember anything specific. My only recollection from hearing my parents discuss him was that he skated on the wrong side of the law. That was enough for Dad—' She broke off catching her breath. 'My father was so law-abiding. He never even had a parking ticket, which is one of the reasons I've always believed he was innocent.'

'Does that mean you can't think of any reason why your mother would have made regular weekly payments to her cousin?' Seb asked.

Daryl exhaled loudly. 'Well, all I can think of is that he was in some kind of financial mess and begged her for help. Mum always wanted to help the underdog... But considering how my father felt about Gordon, I can't really understand it... I'm sorry I can't be of more help.'

'On the contrary, this is very useful,' Birdie assured her. 'Do you know where we can find him? Is he still alive?'

'As far as I know, he is. The last I heard, he was living in Northampton.'

'You don't have a photo of him by any chance, do you?' Birdie asked.

'No... Wait. Yes, there's one from a Christmas when he turned up drunk on the doorstep. Dad didn't want him to come inside but Mum couldn't turn him away. I'll take a photo of it and text it to you.'

'Excellent. Thank you. I'd also like to ask you about Rosemary Fry, the neighbour from across the road who made the initial statement incriminating your father. What was her relationship like with your parents?' Seb asked.

'They were on nodding terms, that's all. It's quite a busy road and we didn't see much of her. I don't recall my mother mentioning her as a friend. I wasn't allowed to attend court, so didn't hear what she said while being questioned.'

'Was there any tension between Rosemary and Kerry after the trial?' Seb asked.

'Not that I know of. Kerry didn't talk about it.'

'Did Kerry believe that your dad was guilty?' Birdie asked.

'This will sound strange, but it wasn't discussed. Kerry was more concerned with us all moving forward after Mum died.'

'I understand,' Birdie said. 'Back to Rosemary. What can you tell us about her?'

'She stayed in the same house until a few years ago when she moved to Wolverhampton to live with her daughter.'

'Were the two of you friendly?' Birdie asked, frowning.

'We'd speak if we bumped into each other in the street. I can text you her new address and phone number, if you'd like it.'

'Yes, please,' Seb said. 'How come you have it?'

'I'm not sure, you know... I just do.'

'That's fine. Sorry for disturbing your evening,' Seb said.

'It's not a problem if it means you're progressing with the case,' Daryl said.

Seb ended the call and turned to Birdie and Keira, who were both staring in his direction.

'I take it our next step is finding Gordon Black?' Keira said, her eyes sparkling.

'Correct,' Seb responded.

'You can leave that to me,' Birdie said, returning to her desk and attacking the keyboard.

While Birdie worked, Seb phoned Rosemary Fry to arrange a time to visit, but there was no answer, and then he went through a set of older bank statements, to check if there were any earlier payments to Black, but there were none. He was about to finish for the evening when Birdie's voice disturbed him.

'Result. Gordon Black still lives in Northampton. I found a short article about him in a local paper. He was convicted of grievous bodily harm after an incident at a pub in Daventry. He served time in prison. I've also got an address and a blurred photograph, which looks like it was taken at least fifteen years ago.'

'We'll pay him a visit tomorrow before we see Freda Bryant,' Seb suggested. 'I don't recommend we call first.'

'Definitely not. He sounds like a right slippery fish. A surprise visit will be the best way to get answers.'

TWELVE

Tuesday, 22 July

Birdie's mouth watered as she stood in the queue of her favourite bakery the following morning. Ever since she'd started saving to buy a house, she tried to limit herself to the occasional takeaway and night out with her friends. But after finding her brothers had not only left a war zone in the kitchen when she'd gone downstairs for breakfast, but had also finished her favourite cereal and eaten all the bread, she decided to stop for something to eat instead. Although they'd promised to restock the cereal and bread after cleaning up the mess, she didn't have time to wait. Besides, the occasional cinnamon roll wouldn't hurt anyone.

'Hello, stranger,' a voice called out. Birdie turned as her friend Annie and her cousin Melinda joined her. 'Last time I saw you, you were attempting to climb up on a table to dance.'

'It was Tina Turner. How could I not?' Birdie grinned at them both. 'Thanks for a great night. How are you both?'

'Busting for the loo,' Annie admitted. 'I won't be a moment.

Mel's starting a new job tomorrow, so we're having a celebration breakfast.'

'It's my treat, so you go and I'll order,' Melinda said in a soft voice. Once Annie had disappeared, she turned to Birdie. 'She's been such a big help since I moved here. It's the least I can do.'

'Yeah, she's great. Not to mention an awesome wicket keeper,' Birdie agreed as the queue moved forward. 'What's your new job? I didn't realise you lived here now. I thought you were visiting for Annie's birthday.'

'I've been living in London and really hated how busy it was. Annie suggested I move up here to be with her. I'm a librarian and there aren't loads of jobs but I started looking... and well, here I am.'

'A librarian?' Birdie said, not sure why she was so surprised. Maybe it was because Annie worked in sales and was a self-declared loudmouth. Then again, Melinda seemed a lot shyer than her outgoing cousin. 'Well, congratulations. I don't read as much as I should. I'll have to remember to come by sometime.'

'I'd like that.' Colour hit her cheeks. 'Umm...I actually rang you yesterday.'

'You did?' Birdie said before recalling the missed calls from the unknown number she'd picked up in the car. 'That was you? How did you get my number and why didn't you leave a message?'

'I guess I chickened out... Annie gave it to me. I was calling to see if you'd like to go out for a drink with me one night.' The words all came out in a rush, and Birdie's confusion grew. If she wanted to go for a drink, why not just say so? Or—

Oh. Understanding hit her. Melinda was asking her out on a date.

Birdie had never hidden that she was bisexual, but with so much going on in her life over the last few years, it had been ages since she'd dated seriously. Or even thought about it.

'Sorry, I didn't mean to make you uncomfortable,' Melinda rushed out.

'No, it's not that,' Birdie told her firmly. 'It caught me by surprise, that's all. I'm in the middle of a case right now and tend to get a bit single-minded. Can I get back to you?'

'Of course,' Melinda agreed calmly, causing Birdie to realise that while she might look shy, she was also self-assured.

Despite herself, Birdie's gaze swept over Melinda again. She was wearing a long denim skirt and a floral blouse that were teamed up with a pair of cherry Doc Martens. Her straight brown hair fell behind her shoulders, and a sprinkle of freckles dotted her nose, while her brown eyes were fringed with dark lashes.

Definitely cute.

'Next,' the guy behind the counter called out as Annie reappeared and joined them.

'Good luck with the new job and I'll be in touch. Okay?' Birdie caught Melinda's eye.

'Sure. No pressure.'

Birdie grinned as she gave her order, including something for Keira and Seb, and once she'd paid, she headed back to her car.

She made the short journey to East Farndon, where Seb was waiting. They usually took his car when they had to travel, but since she now had a company car that was large enough to take his giant frame and didn't rattle and hiss whenever she drove on the motorway, she suggested they take hers.

'Fine by me,' he agreed, and forty minutes later they were coming off Castle Avenue, Duston, the area of Northampton where Gordon Black lived. She pulled into a car park at the rear of a block of council flats.

'Is everything okay? You seem a little distracted?' Seb asked as they walked across the uneven concrete path.

'Um, yes. I've just been thinking about the case.' Birdie

quickly shook her head. Despite her forthright personality, when it came to her personal life, she wasn't much of a sharer. Especially since she hadn't yet decided what to do about Melinda's invitation.

Which was weird. When she was younger, Birdie wouldn't think twice about agreeing to go out with someone if she liked them, but the fact that Melinda was her friend's cousin, meant things could quickly get awkward if it didn't work out. Cricket was her stress release and she didn't want to ruin it.

Yet, the idea of going on a date made her smile.

'There's a lot to think about,' Seb agreed casually, though she wasn't sure he believed her. Not that he'd ever push, which she appreciated. 'Here we are. Number five.'

It was a ground-floor flat, with one window overlooking the path, and a faded blue door. Through the net curtains, a television flickered, and Birdie could just make out the sound of a game show.

'It looks like we're in luck. He's got the telly on.'

Seb pressed the doorbell. There was no sound and so he followed it up with a sharp rap on the door.

'Hold your bloody horses,' a voice grumbled from somewhere inside.

There was a shuffling sound and then the clink of a key turning before the door opened to reveal a short man in his late sixties or early seventies. His nose was veiny and red, and his skin was lined from what Birdie suspected was too many nights in the pub. His eyes were narrowed and calculating. He ran a scarred hand through his unwashed hair. There was little resemblance to the photograph Birdie found of him, or the one that Daryl had sent through the previous evening.

'Mr Black?' Birdie asked.

'Who the hell are you?' he demanded, not bothering to answer Birdie's question. His sharp gaze swept over them. 'If it's about money, you can fuck off.'

'We're not debt collectors. Are you Gordon Black?' Birdie repeated as Seb inched a foot into the door frame.

'That depends.' He glanced down at Seb's foot and then up to his looming figure. Some of the bravado left him and he shrugged. 'Yeah. What's it to you?'

'I'm Birdie, and this is Sebastian Clifford. We're private investigators and would like to talk to you about your cousin Helen Brackstone.'

His posture shifted, but his eyes gleamed. He grunted and gestured for them to follow him inside. 'I'd offer you a cuppa, but the milk's gone off,' he muttered before disappearing towards the sound of the television.

The flat was tiny, and the hallway was cluttered with shoes, dirty clothing and an assortment of boxes that appeared to contain electrical goods... Was he handling stolen goods?

The sitting room was equally messy and the large telly was surrounded by piles of newspapers, as well as discarded pizza boxes and takeaway containers. In the corner, there was another pile of unopened boxes... More black market goods, she suspected. Not that she was going to ask him; they had more pressing matters to discuss.

Black sank into a grubby maroon leather armchair and waved an arm at two mismatched dining-room chairs. Birdie dragged them closer to the man and Seb picked up the remote control and muted the TV.

'You don't mind, do you?' Seb asked.

'Course not. Come in and take over,' Black retorted before picking up a vape stick and taking a drag. 'If you two are investigators, I take it you know that my cousin died years ago.'

'We do,' Seb said. 'We're looking into the events leading up to her death and wanted to ask you about the payments she made to you.'

Birdie admired his restraint; after five minutes in Black's

company, she already wanted to give him what for... Figuratively speaking, of course.

'Payments?' He sucked on his vape again and exhaled. The room filled with the sickly sweet scent of strawberries. 'No idea what you're talking about.'

Birdie clenched her fists, but Seb leant back and crossed his long legs, as if he was having a casual chat with a friend.

'Let me jog your memory. From June 1988 through to April 1989, you received weekly payments of thirty pounds. Also in 1988, there were a further six payments of four hundred and fifty pounds each, bringing the total Helen paid you to just over four thousand pounds. If you consider that inflation has averaged three point three per cent over the years, it means that today, it would have been the equivalent of approximately ten thousand pounds.'

Black blinked and gave Birdie a questioning glance. 'What's with Supercomputer, here?'

'Just one of his *many* talents,' Birdie said, with a shrug. 'Why did Helen pay you so much money when, according to her daughter, you'd never been close and her husband actively disliked you?'

'Wes Brackstone was a twat.' Black scowled. 'And since he was also a cold-blooded killer, I didn't lose any sleep over it. As for us not being close, we got on fine. Helen was family. She was the only one not to turn her back on me when I hit a rough patch.'

'You're saying she paid you this money each week because she felt sorry for you?' Birdie didn't bother to hide her scepticism.

'Not all of us are born with a silver spoon like this one.' He nodded at Seb, who, even in his more casual attire, still looked like he'd stepped off the pages of *Vanity Fair* magazine. 'There's no shame in asking for help, is there?'

'Of course not. You were lucky you had such an obliging

cousin who could afford to be so generous.' Seb uncrossed his legs and leant forward. 'What I find interesting, though, is that there were no payments in May... Which just happened to be two weeks before Helen's death.'

'Weird what sort of things keeps a person up at night,' Black responded.

'It didn't keep *you* up at night, then? Not even when you were going through a "rough patch" and suddenly found yourself thirty quid down each week? That's quite a chunk,' Birdie said. 'Surely you had some thoughts about it.'

He gritted his teeth. 'All right, I was pissed off. But I figured her husband had found out and stopped her.'

'Did you ask her?' Seb asked.

'What was the point? It was lucky I didn't, I reckon, or else it could've been me that the maniac poisoned.'

Birdie's skin crawled with dislike.

'If Helen was living with a man like that, why would she risk giving you money? There must have been another reason,' she pushed.

'Well, there wasn't,' Black snapped. 'Then again, it was a long time ago and hard for me to remember. Maybe a little, you know, *encouragement*, might help.'

The man's calculating demeanour and lack of remorse were pressing all kinds of buttons for Birdie.

'Is that why Helen paid you? To *"encourage"* you to remember something? Or to forget about it?' Seb asked, locking eyes with Black.

With Black's refusal to answer any questions, Birdie was beginning to suspect that they were dealing with blackmail.

'The only thing she was encouraging me to do was live a better life,' Black replied, smirking.

'Except she stopped the payments. That must have been hard,' Birdie said. 'Here's a thought... You tried phoning when your payment at the beginning of May didn't come through, but

Helen either didn't answer, or worse told you she wasn't going to pay you another penny. It must have made you so hopping mad that you drove the eighteen miles to Market Harborough to confront her, making sure it was at a time when Wes wasn't there.'

'Nice story... but that's all it is,' Black snarled, turning up his lip.

'You don't strike me as someone who'd let a good thing go without fighting for it,' Birdie continued.

'I agree,' Seb said, taking over. 'I suggest that you went to your cousin's house, hoping you could convince her to change her mind, but she refused to listen and you lost your temper and—'

'Whoa,' Black interrupted. He held up his grubby hands. 'Don't you start accusing me of killing her. I'm not like that.'

'You have a record for grievous bodily harm. You *are* like that,' Birdie said. 'I agree with my partner; you visited Helen on the fifteenth of May, argued with her, lost your temper and decided to teach them both a lesson. You killed Helen and set up Wes.'

'You're talking rubbish,' Black muttered, sinking further back in his chair. 'Get out,' he shouted, pointing at the door.

They left, not needing to be asked twice, and the volume of the television rose behind them. Once they were outside in the fresh air, Birdie let out a furious growl.

Birdie peered back towards Black's grimy ground-floor window in time to see the net curtains flutter back into place. He'd been watching them leave.

They headed back to the car.

'What a piece of work,' she said as she slammed the door behind her.

'A most obnoxious man,' Seb agreed. 'Now that we've met him, I can easily believe that he was capable of blackmail and quite possibly worse.'

Birdie started the engine and began driving towards Lutterworth and their appointment with Maurice Bryant's widow, Freda.

'The question is... *what* was he blackmailing Helen over and what did he do when the payments stopped? Being her cousin suggests that she would have let him into the house the day she was killed. We know he's violent, so it's not a stretch to imagine him forcing her to drink poison.'

'But was he clever enough to devise a plan to set up Wes at the same time?' Seb asked. 'But I'm not convinced he'd use poison as a means of killing someone. There are easier ways. And remember the door had been forced, even though we don't know that happened at the time of the murder.'

'Yeah, you could be right,' Birdie agreed as she joined the M1. 'But he also strikes me as an opportunist and he's left me with more questions than answers. Why don't you call Keira and see what else she can dig up on him?'

Seb made the call as Birdie overtook an ancient Reliant Robin that was in the slow lane and they sped towards their next interview. If Keira could find something concrete on him, it would help join the dots.

THIRTEEN

Tuesday, 22 July

'Another day, another retirement home,' Birdie quipped as she pulled into a car park and peered at the sprawling property. 'Although this looks more like a hotel.'

'Retirement *community*,' Seb corrected as he climbed out. 'According to the website, it's all about lifestyle and hobbies.'

'I suppose visiting these places is part of the deal with cold cases... Hey, look, there's a croquet lawn and two tennis courts... Oh, and is that a hedged maze?'

'Yes, though it's overlooked by the apartment buildings, so it would be hard for anyone to get too lost in it.' Seb's phone rang. 'It's Keira,' he said before answering. 'Good timing, you caught us just before we went in to visit Freda Bryant. I'm putting you on speaker.'

'Cool. Hi, Birdie.' Seb held the phone in his palm so they could both speak.

'Hi. Any joy with Black?' Birdie asked.

'Maybe. I've sent through a photograph to see what you think. It was in one of the articles about TEC. Remember Mark

Grant was arrested for throwing red paint at a minister? Well,' she continued, not waiting for an answer. 'I was going through different photos used in newspaper reports of the incident, and I'm almost certain Helen was in one of them. That means she was there at the time.'

'Really?' Birdie said.

'Yes. I can't be a hundred per cent certain because the halftone dots make it hard to confirm it.'

'Halftone dots? What's that when it's at home?' Birdie turned to Seb.

'It's the process that turns the images into patterns of small and large dots before being converted into a negative and exposed to light sensitive emulsion,' he said.

'Of course it is.' Birdie blinked, none the wiser.

'There's something else,' Keira added. 'Not far from her is someone who looks like Black. And – get a load of this – Maurice Bryant is also nearby. It's hard to tell if they're together or not. Or, if it's even them,' she added, suddenly sounding doubtful. 'Maybe I just wanted it to be them?'

'Everything starts with a hunch,' Seb assured her.

'That's right,' Birdie agreed. 'Can you send the photo through?'

'Already have. You should get it any time now,' Keira said as Birdie's phone pinged, quickly followed by Seb's.

'It's here.' Birdie swiped through to the attachment to bring it up.

'Great. I'll let you go,' Keira said. 'If you want to get a growing girl some afternoon tea on the way back, don't let me stop you.'

They ended the call, and Birdie and Seb silently studied the photo on their respective phones. It was a blurred image of greys and whites, showing several policemen holding back a crowd of about twenty people. It was hard to separate any faces in the crowd, and Birdie used her fingers to expand it on her screen. But the closer in she went, the more the image turned into a distorted jumble of dots. Now she understood Seb's explanation of the process.

She zoomed out again and held the image further away, managing to make out the image of Helen, her dark hair and eyes almost identical to Daryl's. To the left was a man with the same narrow eyes as Black, and to the right, but behind her shoulder, was a second man with broad shoulders and short hair. It could easily have been Bryant.

'While I wouldn't want to bet money on us seeing Helen, Bryant and Black together, we can certainly mention it to Freda,' Birdie said. 'What was Black doing there? Even if he wasn't with Helen on the day, it's ringing all sorts of alarm bells. For all we know, he could've been in league with Maurice Bryant?'

'That's possible, but we need to be cognisant of the fact that the event in question took place in August 1988, which was two months *after* Helen began making regular payments to Black,' Seb said.

'I love that mind of yours... except when you mess with my ideas,' Birdie said with a grimace, which was quickly followed by a grin.

'Freda might be able to shed some light on it,' Seb said, giving her a wry smile as they made their way into the reception area.

The country club feel of the place continued, with marbled floors and a gleaming reception counter.

'Off you go, Prince Charming,' Birdie teased, ushering Seb in the direction of reception. It was funny to see his discomfort when she went on about the effect he had on people.

But he merely raised an eyebrow in her direction and then strode across to the long desk. After a quick conversation, he rejoined her and nodded in the direction of the stairwell.

'Freda's in apartment twenty-one on the third floor. You'll

be pleased to know it overlooks the croquet lawn. The receptionist rang ahead to let her know that we're on our way.'

'Excellent.' Birdie took the stairs two at a time. She didn't always have time to visit the gym while they were working a case, so liked to take the opportunity to get in some exercise. Her feet echoed on the steps and her heart was pounding as they stepped out onto the third floor.

She knocked twice, and after a clicking noise, the door opened automatically. On the other side was an elderly woman in a wheelchair, holding a small remote control. Her fingers were swollen and misshapen with arthritis, but her hair was a startling blue and that matched her twinkling eyes.

'Come in.' She waved them through, pressed the remote again, and the door closed behind them.

'Thank you for agreeing to see us. I'm Birdie and this is my partner, Seb. We're private investigators and would like to ask you some questions about your husband, Maurice.'

At the mention of her husband's name, Freda's eyes turned expressive. 'Whatever you're working on must have happened a long time ago. My Maurice has been dead for thirty-six years.'

'Yes, so we understand,' Seb said. 'I hope you don't mind our intrusion.'

'Not at all. I don't get to talk about him much these days – apart from to myself.' She chuckled. 'Come through to my lounge and let's get comfortable.'

Freda turned her chair and led them through to a bright room that was flooded with afternoon sunlight from the wide glass doors that opened out onto a balcony filled with plants. Again, Birdie had apartment envy.

'What a lovely place,' Birdie said.

'It is rather, isn't it?' Freda indicated for them to sit on the sofa while she transferred herself into an easy chair. Seb went to help her, but she shook her head. 'It's okay. I've mastered the art over the years, and it's important I don't allow my muscles to weaken.'

'How long have you been in the chair?' Seb asked.

'Ten years.' She held out her hands. 'I have rheumatoid arthritis and my children were worried about me living on my own, especially as none of them lived close by, which is why I moved here. I enjoy it; there's plenty to do, and as you can see, there's nothing wrong with me up top.' She tapped her bright hair and gave them a cheeky smile. 'Would one of you like to go into the kitchen and bring through the tea and biscuits I got ready?'

'I'll do it.' Birdie jumped up and headed out the door and into the kitchen, where she found a tray. She poured out three cups of tea and carried everything back into the lounge.

'Biscuit?' Birdie asked, offering the plate to their host after handing out the cups of tea.

'Yes, please. It's not tea without a biscuit.' Freda took one with a shaking hand and then Birdie sat down. 'Now, what would you like to know?'

'We're looking into the murder of Helen Brackstone,' Birdie said.

If the name was familiar, Freda didn't show it.

'I'm sorry, it's not ringing any bells.'

'It happened on the fifteenth of May, 1989. Helen was a married mother of one who was poisoned in her home in Market Harborough.'

Freda's mouth trembled, and a shadow crossed her face. 'I don't recall anything about it. But I do know that year all too well. You see, Maurice died on the fifteenth of July.'

'Would you mind telling us how he died?' Birdie asked, gently.

'They said it was a heart attack... but... it came so out of the blue. Yes, he was a little overweight and occasionally had a drink, but that was all. The coroner said it was down to his lifestyle.' Freda's mouth was tight.

'Did you agree?' Birdie gently pushed, hoping she was reading Freda's reaction correctly.

The older woman let out a sigh. 'I'm no doctor, but it was hard to get my head around it at the time because he'd shown no signs of illness. One day we were happy and the next—' She broke off, her voice choked with emotion. 'Well... never mind. It all happened a long time ago.'

Birdie was silent, not wanting to intrude on her grief. After several moments of silence, Seb shifted in his seat and placed his cup and saucer on the tray.

'I realise you don't remember Helen Brackstone's murder, but did Maurice ever mention her name?' Seb asked.

'Not that I recall.' The older woman frowned. 'Why would he? You're not trying to say that he had anything—'

'No, nothing like that,' Birdie quickly cut in. 'Helen was involved in a group called The Equality Collective that was based out of Leicester.'

'Ah.' Understanding filled Freda's blue eyes and she nodded. 'TEC. Now that's something I do remember. They caused all manner of trouble. Maurice couldn't join them, if that's what you were thinking, because he'd have lost his job if his bosses found out. Back then, no one wanted radicals causing problems in the office, and we had a young family to consider.'

'Are you saying that he was sympathetic to their cause?' Seb questioned, sounding neutral, as if not wanting to lead her.

'I'm not sure he was sympathetic to *all* their actions, especially the riots and protests that stopped traffic, which seemed very chaotic. But he was a man of principle and agreed with some of what they campaigned for – we both did – but we believed change should come from within.'

'Change from the inside?' Seb reiterated.

'Yes, that's exactly it. I was a teacher and Maurice a town planner, as you probably know.'

'Yes, we do,' Seb said. 'What can you tell us about his job?'

'Maurice worked in various council departments before moving into planning. He had a knack for technical drawing and worked his way up the ranks. It's different these days, but back then, town planning was only starting to be viewed as a career.'

'Did he enjoy it?' Birdie asked.

'At first, he did. He saw it as a chance to shape the future for the next generation. To leave things better than he found them. But he quickly became disillusioned with his boss.' Freda sighed. 'Maurice couldn't prove anything, but he believed the man was taking bribes to approve certain projects and refuse others.'

Birdie jotted everything down. It appeared that Maurice might have been an informant, rather than someone TEC might target.

'Do you remember the name of his boss?' she asked.

'Tony Lucas. He wore expensive suits that were way above his paygrade... At least that's what Maurice said.'

'Did he ever mention what projects were given the green light by Lucas?' Birdie asked.

Freda took a bite of her biscuit and shook her head. 'No, like I said, Maurice was very principled, and I think he felt guilty for even mentioning it to me.'

'What about a company called Fullerton Construction? They were property developers back when he would've been working in the planning office,' Birdie asked.

Again, Freda shook her head. 'No, but I know the mob you mean. They were responsible for that dreadful Camberton Towers. There was a huge ruckus at the time because they flattened a housing estate. It happened after Maurice's death, and I remember thinking how upset he'd have been about it.'

'Clearly Maurice believed in social justice. Do you believe it's possible that he leaked information to TEC regarding Lucas and possible corruption inside the planning office?' Seb asked, leaning forward slightly in his chair and looking directly at Freda.

Freda stared back at him, her gaze thoughtful. Then she nodded. 'I can't say for certain, but if he thought it was for the public good, Maurice might have done.'

'We've been hired to investigate Helen's murder. At the time, her husband was charged, and he later died in prison. But no one ever questioned Helen's involvement with TEC and what she was working on. We think she might have been trying to expose Fullerton Construction for bribing the council to pass their plans for building Camberton Towers. We found the initials *MB* written next to some of her notes.'

'Maurice Bryant. I take it you came here, unsure if he was the good guy or the bad guy,' Freda said, giving a half-smile. 'Told you – my body might be a little bent, but my mind works just fine.'

'We are careful not to jump to any conclusions,' Seb said. 'We wanted to follow it up as a possible lead. I hope our questions haven't upset you.'

'Upset me? Goodness no. It's the most interesting thing that's happened in a long time. Maurice was a good man, and it makes me happy to know that he might have done his bit to help. And in case you're wondering, he wouldn't have leaked information for money.' She paused for a moment. 'You don't think that... no, that's ridiculous...'

'What is it?' Birdie asked.

'Maurice died so young... Could it have been something to do with this...? No... It was his heart.'

Birdie swallowed. It was one thing to believe that Maurice's death wasn't coincidental, but it was another to imply it to his widow. But it also wasn't fair to not answer her question.

'We have no reason to think so at the moment, but if we discover anything to the contrary, we'll let you know.'

'Thank you, dear.'

'Do you know someone called Gordon Black, or did Maurice ever mention the name?' Seb asked, moving the conversation on.

'No, I don't think so.'

'I have a photo of him.' Seb passed over his phone, with the image of Black that Birdie had discovered yesterday.

Freda fumbled with a pair of reading glasses and studied it for a few seconds before shaking her head. 'He doesn't look familiar.'

'That's okay.' Birdie brought up the photo that Keira had discovered and crouched down beside Freda to show her. 'We also found this. Is that Maurice in the crowd?'

This time Freda let out a soft sigh and her finger traced the screen. 'Oh, yes, that's him. I remember this happening. Maurice worked on the project but wasn't a fan of the minister who opened the building. He didn't approve of the paint throwing, but was pleased to have been in the paper. I still have my own copy, though it's faded a lot now.'

Birdie repressed a smile. Keira would be delighted to know she'd been right about Bryant being there.

'To the left of Maurice is Helen Brackstone, and in the next group of people is Gordon Black,' Birdie said, pointing to the man in question.

Freda studied it for several more seconds before looking up. 'I still don't recognise him. Sorry. I wish I could be of more help.'

'It's the total opposite. You've been a great help,' Birdie said with a smile.

'Thank you.' However, a troubled expression crossed her face. 'But now I keep thinking that somehow Maurice's death wasn't a heart attack.'

'It's important not to speculate,' Seb stated. 'If anything in our investigation suggests that's the case, we'll refer it to the police, and we'll let you know, as Birdie has already said. Thank you for your time and assistance.'

'It's been a pleasure. I've enjoyed your company. I won't get back into my wheelchair to see you out, if you don't mind.'

'Of course not,' Birdie assured her. 'But we'll take everything back to the kitchen first.'

After leaving the retirement community, Birdie drove down the drive and turned onto the road to East Farndon. 'Freda wasn't joking about having all her marbles. I'd sort of hoped she wouldn't work out that Maurice's death could have been suspicious as we don't have any proof.'

'Agreed. And she appears to have approved of any possible involvement he had with TEC.'

'We need to confirm whether he really was passing information to Helen, so TEC could bring down Lucas and Fullerton Construction,' Birdie said.

'We must also investigate Tony Lucus further. To check if he had any links with Fullerton Construction, and was involved in other planning decisions benefitting property developers in the wider community.'

'Black needs looking into further, too,' Birdie added. 'It's entirely possible we can link him to Fullerton Construction or Lucas.'

'Or both.'

'Or both,' Birdie agreed. 'What's the plan? Shall we return to Black's, or let him stew while we research Lucas and Fullerton Construction?'

'Stew,' Seb immediately answered. 'He doesn't strike me as someone who makes rational decisions. Letting him worry about whether the other shoe is about to drop could well be the most effective way.'

FOURTEEN

Tuesday, 22 July

It was almost three o'clock by the time Seb settled back at his desk. Birdie and Keira were still in the kitchen, where he'd left them discussing ways to enhance the photograph showing Helen, Maurice Bryant and Black in the crowd, so it was clearer.

Keira had mentioned a friend from university who might be able to help, so Seb left Birdie to decide whether it was an avenue worth pursuing. Instead, he turned his attention to Tony Lucas, Maurice Bryant's boss at the planning office.

They'd worked together well before the internet was around, and it took several searches before Seb came up with a death notice for an Anthony John Lucas who was born in 1949 and died in 2015. It was followed by a small obituary.

Anthony Lucas – known by everyone as Tony – was a long-time town planner credited with helping Leicester's urban revival. His tireless work for the city that he loved was recognised when he received an OBE. Having lost his wife five years ago, and with no children, his legacy lives on in the city itself.

Seb frowned as Birdie burst into the room, causing a sleeping Elsa to slowly open an eye.

'Keira's contacting her friend about the photo,' Birdie said, rushing to Seb's desk and leaning over his shoulder to read his screen. 'Crap. Lucas is dead? How annoying of him.'

'Yes, most inconvenient.' Seb scrolled further down the page to show her an image of the man. This was taken in 1995, which would have made him forty-six at the time. But with his shock of white hair, wide face, and heavy jowls, he could've passed as twenty years older.

'At least we now know what he looks like. I'll keeping going through online archives and newspaper articles to see how many times he turns up. There's bound to be loads if he received an OBE. Can an honour like that be taken away posthumously? If he's as guilty as we think he is, it should be.'

'That's a discussion for another time. We don't yet know how deep his involvement is,' Seb replied, wanting to rein in Birdie. She was prone to becoming extremely indignant when faced with injustice, and it needed managing to prevent compromising the case.

'I suppose,' Birdie said, moving away from Seb and sitting at her laptop. 'While you do that, I'll finish going through Helen's boxes.'

While Seb and Birdie worked, Keira's voice drifted through from the kitchen as she spoke on the phone. Hearing the noise, Elsa roused again, this time leaving the room. No doubt she was hoping for a treat. Thankfully, Keira had never fallen victim to Elsa's pleading looks and could be trusted to stick to the Lab's eating schedule.

'What's this?' Birdie asked, holding up a cassette.

Seb glanced over at her. 'It's from a camcorder. Popular in

the 1980s and used to record videos. It goes into a larger cassette and it can then be played in a video player.'

'Yikes. How antiquated. Thank heavens for smartphones because this seems a right faff.'

'We need the larger cassette to play it. Is it in the box?'

'I'll check.' Birdie stuck her head into the box and pulled out a red cardboard container, from which she pulled out the cassette. 'Is this it?'

'It looks like it. Now we need a video player.' Seb frowned. 'Actually, Sarah has one in the old playroom, in the entertainment unit. Come on. We'll collect Keira on the way. Bring the tapes.'

They set up the first video and the three of them sat on the sofa, facing the screen.

The first image was of two men who were standing in the middle of a cricket pitch, both looking very pleased with themselves.

'That's Tony Lucas,' Birdie said. 'You can't mistake him with that white hair. Pause it.' Seb pressed the pause button and they all stared at the screen. The other man was tall and lean with a self-satisfied air about him, putting Seb in mind of someone used to getting their own way.

'Is the man with Lucas, Roger North, the Fullerton MD?' Keira asked.

'I reckon,' Birdie said. 'Press play because I also think they're at Grace Road, where Leicestershire play county cricket.'

Seb resumed the recording and they saw a banner on the edge of the pitch stating that the match was sponsored by Fullerton Construction.

'You're correct,' Seb said, turning to Birdie.

'I can't believe they could have been involved in their dodgy dealing at such a sacred place,' Birdie growled, unable to hide her annoyance at the prospect of her beloved game being tarnished at the well-known ground.

'If Fullerton was a sponsor, they would have had a corporate box, which suggests Lucas was one of their guests for the day,' Seb suggested.

'A perk for pushing through their application, I bet.' Birdie's knuckles whitened as she continued staring at the TV. 'It proves there's a connection between the pair, which means Maurice Bryant's suspicions about his boss are probably correct.'

'Keira, can you stay here and go through the tapes to see if there's anything else that's useful while we go back to the office to see what else we can find on North,' Seb said.

'Sure,' Keira said.

Seb and Birdie returned to the office and began their search.

'Over here,' Birdie said after twenty minutes.

Seb dragged his chair over. Sure enough, her screen soon filled with image after image of the smug-looking businessman. Most of them taken at social events, charity functions and even a royal wedding.

'He got around a bit, didn't he?' Birdie muttered. 'Is there any chance your parents would know him?'

Seb doubted it. Even though it was clear North rubbed shoulders with many people, it was far from meaning he was in the same social circle as them.

'I've never heard them mention him by name, but I'll call tonight to check.' He stood up and retrieved his phone from the desk. 'I'm going to try contacting Rosemary Fry again to arrange for us to visit her in Wolverhampton.'

'How annoying that she's not answering. Maybe she's gone away for a few days?'

'That's certainly a possibility, which is why I'm not prepared to drive seventy miles on the off chance she's there. We need to arrange the interview,' Seb said.

'While you're doing that, I'll see if I can find a link between North and Black.'

Seb headed over to the French doors and opened them, letting in the warmth of the day. He then called Rosemary Fry, but, yet again, it went straight to voicemail. He left another message and headed back to his desk.

'I've just text you both a copy of the photo,' Keira said, walking into the office. 'My friend just sent it to me. The images are much clearer now. I've gone through the tapes, on fast forward. There was a bit more at the cricket match and the others were blank.'

'Maybe Helen had only just started recording stuff. Thanks for the photo, it makes up for the fact I can't find anything linking Black and North,' Birdie said with a sigh. 'Then again, if there was a connection, I can't imagine someone like Roger North wanting to advertise it. I reckon we should pay Black another visit tomorrow. He might have clocked my car from our last visit, so we'll go in yours – we don't want him forewarned.'

FIFTEEN

Wednesday, 23 July

Black's reaction as he opened the front door the following morning was every bit as sullen as Seb had expected.

'What the hell?' Black muttered, trying to peer past Seb's shoulder.

'You don't look pleased to see us.' Birdie peered through the front door and let out a whistle. 'Yet you must have been expecting someone if you've tidied up. What happened to the "mess"?'

'I don't have to let you in, you know. You're not police.' Black poked out his lower lip in a belligerent pout.

'That's correct. We're more than happy to discuss this on the doorstep, aren't we, Seb?' Birdie smirked.

'More than happy,' Seb acknowledged, raising his voice so the neighbours could hear.

A flicker of annoyance crossed Black's face, and he grudgingly stepped to the side.

'Okay, okay, I get what you're doing. Come inside, but it won't do any good. I told you everything yesterday.'

'We'll see about that,' Birdie said as she pushed her way past him.

The stuffy lounge no longer resembled a makeshift warehouse, and while the takeaway containers and dirty clothes were still strewn around the place, along with the dank stench, there was no sign of any illegal activity.

'How do you know Maurice Bryant?' Birdie asked once they were all seated.

'Who?' Black replied, his eyes narrowed.

Seb pulled out his phone and brought up the photo that Keira had sent him. Black's face was clearly visible, and it was obvious his focus wasn't on his cousin, Helen, but on Maurice Bryant. He held it up so that Black could see. 'This might jog your memory.'

'You'll notice that Helen's there, too,' Birdie added. 'This was taken two months after she started paying you. Remember the payments? The ones that stopped two weeks before her death? You do get where we're going with this, don't you?'

Black scowled and shifted awkwardly in his chair. 'Fine. Helen was paying me a few quid to keep my mouth shut. It's not illegal.'

'That's incorrect,' Seb said. 'Blackmail is most definitely illegal.'

'Who said it was blackmail?' Black said, unable to look either of them in the eye.

'We do,' Birdie said. 'What did you have on Helen?'

Black's jaw clenched. 'I was living in Leicester at the time, and one day, I saw Helen in a fancy café not far from the council buildings. She was having an intense conversation with some guy.'

'What guy?' Birdie cut in.

'Him. The one in the photo. Bryant.' Black jabbed his finger in the direction of Seb's phone.

'Having a chat with someone isn't enough to blackmail them. Did you go inside and overhear something?'

'No, because she'd have seen me. I waited across the street for her to leave and followed her back to her car. You should have seen how red her cheeks went when she saw me. At the time, I figured she'd been having a fling and I'd caught them.'

'Did you accuse her of having an affair and threaten to tell Wes if she didn't pay you?' Seb asked, pocketing his phone and folding his arms.

'I was skint, and it was easy money. It was nothing against Helen,' Black replied.

'It was everything against Helen,' Birdie said, leaning forward, her red curls seeming to spring up to match her mood. 'What better way to show your fondness for a person than blackmailing them? What did Helen say when you accused her?'

'She denied it and was upset by my accusation. I told her she was lying. Eventually she admitted that Bryant worked at the council, and he was helping her with some TEC stuff.'

Seb frowned. Why would Helen admit that to Black? It made no sense. Birdie's brow puckered, suggesting she'd come to the same conclusion.

'I don't buy it. Helen wouldn't tell you what was going on between her and Bryant,' Birdie said.

'Well, that's where you're wrong. Me and Helen were cool. She was big on fighting injustice and helping the underdog. And you don't get more underdog than me. She wanted me to join the group, but I wasn't interested. They were sitting ducks for being arrested and I didn't need that.'

'So, she wanted to help you, and in return, you blackmailed her,' Birdie said with a frustrated sigh. 'I bet she loved you for that.'

There was no smart retort or protest this time. Instead, Black shrugged. 'She had no choice because I threatened to leak it to the media that Bryant was part of TEC. Back then, the tabloids were always happy to cough up for a juicy story.'

'What if you had told the media?' Birdie asked, giving Black a stony glare.

'Helen told me it would ruin everything. She needed Bryant at the council because he still hadn't found all the evidence she needed.'

'Why did you attend the rally where the photograph was taken then? Were you keeping tabs on her?' Seb asked, trying to piece it all together.

'Yeah. I wanted Helen to know that she couldn't hide anything from me.'

'If Helen was paying you money to keep quiet,' Seb said, leaning forward and resting his elbows on his knees, 'why did the payments stop, and what action did you take when they did?'

Sweat beaded on the man's forehead and he wiped it away with a grimy sleeve. 'Well, I can tell you now, I was really pissed off. I went to see her and told her I needed the money, but she said that Wes had found out about it and was making her stop. She said they had a huge row that got so loud one of the neighbours called the police.'

Seb nodded at Birdie. The argument tied in with the domestic-violence report that had been in Dunbar's old police notebooks.

'Two weeks after she stopped paying you, Helen ended up dead. What do you have to say about that?' Birdie asked.

'No comment.' Black sat upright in his chair and folded his arms tightly across his chest.

'This isn't a police interview,' Birdie snapped. 'If you had nothing to do with Helen's death, then who did?'

'It was Wes.'

Birdie gave a loud sigh. 'We don't know that. What did you do after the money stopped?'

Black's eyes darted between Seb and Birdie.

'Okay, I'll tell you the truth... if you believe that I didn't kill Helen.'

'We're listening...' Seb acquiesced.

'I approached Bryant – you know, thinking I could make it a double pay day – and he told me where to get off. He said he'd rather lose his job than give in to blackmail.'

'That must have hurt,' Birdie said.

'You think?' Black muttered.

'What did you do then?' Seb snapped, beginning to lose his patience with the man.

There was silence apart from Black's laboured breathing. Finally, he relaxed his arms.

'Okay. I'll tell you, and then you can bugger off and leave me alone. Because this all happened years ago. I went to Bryant's boss, Tony Lucas, and told him he had a rat on his ship. I said for two hundred quid I'd name names. He paid up and that was the end of it.'

'Except Helen was then murdered. Did you blame yourself?' Birdie asked.

'Why the hell would I?'

'Didn't you think that after you'd told Lucas about Helen and Bryant, that it could have been the reason for her death?'

'No... no. I swear I didn't. Wes was charged and I thought he'd done it,' Black said.

'What about Bryant?' Birdie asked, shaking her head, clearly frustrated by the man's lack of understanding.

'What about him?'

'He died two months after Helen. Apparently, it was a heart attack, but according to his wife, he'd been reasonably healthy with no signs of heart issues before then.'

'What?' The sullen expression disappeared as the colour drained from his face. 'Are you sure?'

'Yes,' Seb said curtly. 'Very sure.'

'I didn't know about that. Or that Wes might not have killed Helen.' Black let out a soft moan and a shadow fell across his face. For the first time since they'd met him, Seb believed what he was saying.

'Did you see Lucas again?' he asked.

'No. The deal was a one-time thing.'

'I see.' Seb traded glances with Birdie and they both stood at the same time. They'd got as much as they could from Black. At least for now.

Seb dropped a card into the man's lap. 'If you remember anything else, call me. And before you ask, no, we won't be paying for information.'

They didn't speak as they returned to where Seb had parked his car. Several groups of people were dotted along the road and they swivelled to watch them, but no one said anything as they climbed in.

Birdie clicked her seatbelt in place. 'Poor Helen, having a cousin like him.'

'We can't pick our family,' Seb reminded her as his phone rang. 'It's Rosemary Fry.'

'Hello?' an elderly voice said from the other end. 'Is this Sebastian Clifford?'

'It is, and you must be Rosemary. I'm a private investigator, as I mentioned in the message I left for you. I was hoping to visit so we could discuss your old neighbour Helen Brackstone.'

'That poor woman. So tragic what happened to her. Yes, I'd be happy to meet with you. I live in Wolverhampton now with my daughter Veronica. Is that okay?'

'Of course. My colleague Birdie and I are happy to drive over. Are you available this afternoon?'

'Umm... This afternoon? I don't think so. Veronica isn't home, and she wouldn't want me seeing you on my own. Would you like to come over tomorrow morning when she's here?'

'That's perfect. We'll be there at ten, if that suits,' Seb said.

Rosemary agreed and gave him the address. Seb didn't explain that Daryl had already given it to them, not wanting her to think they'd been researching into her. He listened patiently and thanked her, before ending the call.

'She has a lot of explaining to do tomorrow. Not least about changing her statement to the police,' Birdie said as Seb started the engine. 'We should also ask her if she noticed Black or Lucas ever visiting the Brackstone house. That's assuming her view wasn't totally obstructed.'

'It's possible that once Lucas discovered Bryant was feeding Helen and TEC information, he paid her a visit,' Seb reasoned. 'Possibly on the day she was poisoned. After all, if he was taking bribes, he had a lot to lose if it was exposed.'

'Yes – and here's a thought – Lucas might have visited Rosemary as well, if he believed that she'd witnessed something. He might have bribed her to change her story to the police?' Birdie said, drumming her fingers on her thigh.

'It does fit. It would mean that Black was inadvertently responsible for Helen's death.'

'Definitely. Whatever he told us about not having anything to do with it, he must have known there would be consequences for his cousin. Lucas paid him well for the information. What did he think was going to happen?'

'There's no point in debating that now,' Seb said as he rejoined the motorway and headed back to East Farndon. 'With Lucas and Bryant both dead, it's time to turn our attention to someone who is still very much alive and living in Switzerland. Roger North.'

SIXTEEN

Thursday, 24 July

Rosemary Fry's daughter Veronica lived ten minutes away from the Wolverhampton ring road in a red-brick semi-detached house. It had a colourful garden at the front, dotted with soft pastel roses, hollyhocks, and hydrangeas. The low hum of bees and the flowers' fragrant scents drifted around them, making Birdie smile. Maybe, she should take up gardening... The trouble was, she'd only ever managed to keep one small cactus alive and had never paid much attention to her mum's own flower beds in the back garden.

Was this a sign that it was time for her to take more notice?

Or maybe she was feeling calmer since having a texting marathon with Melinda last night? She still hadn't decided about the date, but when the librarian had texted her about a new memoir by one of Birdie's favourite cricketers, they'd ended up messaging about books and movies for half the evening.

'You're in a buoyant mood this morning,' Seb stated as they reached the front door.

'It must have been spending an hour and a half in the car with you that did it.' Birdie winked in his direction and rang the bell.

'It's most heartening that you're comfortable enough with me to sing show tunes the entire journey,' he countered, his voice as deadpan and calm as ever.

Birdie waggled a jazz hand in his direction as the door opened and a woman in her late thirties appeared. She had short dark hair and bright hazel eyes, fringed with dark lashes.

'You must be Birdie and Sebastian,' she said. 'I'm Veronica, Rosemary's daughter. I hope you don't mind, but I called Daryl last night to confirm you were who you said you were.'

'No problem,' Birdie said, handing over her business card and shaking Veronica's held-out hand. 'We appreciate your mum agreeing to talk with us.'

Veronica pressed her mouth together, and her eyes clouded. 'Mum loves having visitors and is very friendly. But... I do worry about her. There are so many scams around these days, on the phone, through the internet, and people coming to the front door. It was one of the reasons I convinced her to sell up and move in with us. Plus, it's lovely for her to be around her grandchildren.'

'You'll be pleased to know your mother informed me we could only visit when you were at home,' Seb reassured.

'I'm *very* pleased to hear it.' Some of the worry in Veronica's eyes eased. 'Come in. The children are out with friends today, so we won't be interrupted. Mum's in the front room. Though, please be mindful that it was quite a traumatic time in our lives, and she struggled with knowing that someone from over the road had been murdered.'

'You mentioned contacting Daryl last night. Were you friends at the time of her mother's murder?' Birdie asked.

'Not really, because Daryl's ten years older than me. When

we grew up, we'd chat a bit, and she would check on Mum for me when I couldn't get down to visit, but that was it.'

That would explain why Daryl still had Rosemary's contact details.

Veronica showed them through to the living room, where an elderly woman was sitting in a leather chair with her feet up on a stool.

'Mum, this is Sebastian Clifford. You spoke to him yesterday.'

'I did indeed. Oh, aren't you tall?' Rosemary Fry exclaimed. She was an older version of her daughter, with short silver hair and similar hazel eyes.

'Thank you for agreeing to meet with us.' Seb smiled and sat down on the sofa that Veronica had guided them to. 'This is my partner, Birdie.'

'It's lovely to meet you both. I don't have many visitors. Would you like something to drink? If you've come all the way from Market Harborough, you must be parched. Is coffee okay? Veronica, would you be a dear...?'

'Yes, please, for both of us,' Birdie said with a nod, knowing that Seb would be wanting one, too.

Veronica hurried away and Birdie took out her notebook, giving Rosemary an encouraging smile.

'As Seb explained yesterday, we're looking into Helen's murder, and we hoped you could let us know more about her and Wes. How well did you know them?'

'We weren't close friends, but I knew them well enough to stop for a brief chat when we bumped into each other.'

'What do you know about the marriage?' Birdie asked.

'It seemed fine, but you never know what goes on behind closed doors, obviously. There was one time when the police were called out by one of the neighbours because of a loud argument. But it was something and nothing.'

'You weren't worried about their relationships, then?'

'No. Not at all... Although there was one time when...' Rosemary looked from side to side, as if she was making sure she couldn't be overheard.

'What happened?' Birdie leant forward at the same time as Veronica returned to the room, holding a tray laden with drinks and a plate of cupcakes, which she placed on the table.

'Well, about a year before Helen was— before she died, I bumped into her at the train station. It was on a Saturday and she was on her way to Leicester. She looked guilty, as if she'd been caught doing something wrong. She asked me not to tell Wes I'd seen her there.'

'Did she say why?' Birdie asked.

Rosemary nodded and took the mug of coffee her daughter handed her. 'She told me it was for one of her causes. Helen was always trying to save the world. She worked for a charity, but also did other things. She confided that Wes wasn't happy with the time she spent away from home and the family. That's why she didn't want him to know what she was up to. That day, she'd told him she was going into town shopping.'

Birdie jotted down some notes. So far, everything fitted with what they already knew.

Seb rubbed his chin and gave Rosemary a warm smile. 'Did Wes ever discuss Helen's causes with you?'

'Oh, no. Well... not outright. But it was easy enough to read between the lines. He would sometimes see me pushing Veronica in the pram and would wave. One time, he asked if I minded not working. I was a teacher, but it took so long to get pregnant that when I finally did, I decided to not go back to work until Veronica was older. I remember him staring at Veronica with a wistful expression on his face. It was as if he wanted Helen to be the same as me.'

Birdie tapped her pen against the page. 'Helen only worked

part-time, but she did spend a lot of time on her causes. Do you think Wes resented her job, or the causes?'

'Both,' Rosemary immediately answered. 'Which was silly. Daryl was fourteen at the time, and a good kid. I couldn't see anything wrong with Helen working or becoming involved in something outside of the family. We were in the eighties, not the sixties, for goodness' sake.' Her hands began to knot together in her lap, twisting her wedding ring. 'But when we found out that he'd killed her. I really couldn't believe that he'd go to those lengths and—'

'Mum, don't get yourself upset,' Veronica interrupted, getting to her feet and patting the older woman's arm. 'You can't change the past.'

'You're right. I'm being silly.' She rubbed her daughter's hand on her arm appreciatively. She turned back to the investigators. 'What else would you like to know?'

Veronica's gaze was fixed on Birdie and Seb. She was clearly protective of her mother, which meant Birdie would have to approach the next issue delicately.

'Rosemary, we'd like to ask you a few questions about the day Helen died. We spoke to one of the detectives on the case, and he mentioned that you had several versions of what you saw.'

'I know you're trying to help Daryl, but how can stirring all this up really help?' Veronica's shoulders tightened and she didn't return to her seat.

'It's okay, love.' Rosemary took a deep breath. 'They do have a right to ask... I did make a muddle of it.'

'A muddle?' Veronica's eyes widened. 'You didn't tell me this.'

When Rosemary didn't answer, Birdie nodded back to the seat Veronica had been occupying. 'Please sit down. I promise we're not here to accuse your mother of anything or distress her.

But, back in 1988, she did change her statement a couple of times, and we'd like to find out why.'

'Changed her statement? What do you mean?' Veronica looked first at Birdie and then at Seb.

'The original statement had elements crossed out and replaced. Later, the second set of answers was different to the first,' Seb said evenly.

'Like I said, it was a bit of a muddle. Sit down, love, while I explain,' Rosemary said to her daughter. 'When Helen was found, the police cordoned off the street and visited the neighbours' houses asking questions. I'd been home all morning, and although I hadn't heard anything, I told them that Wes's car was parked in front of the house.'

'Can you remember what time you saw the car and whether you were outside?' Birdie asked.

'What an odd question. Why does it matter where Mum was? Our old house looked directly at theirs.' Veronica bristled, though she didn't stand up again.

'We believe there were trees lining the street at the time that would have made it hard to see the drive.'

'It's true. Lovely old things, they were. I saw Wes's car on my way back from popping round to see the old lady who lived two doors up. I wanted to know if she needed anything from the supermarket,' Rosemary explained, looking more at her daughter than Birdie and Seb. 'The only reason I mentioned it to the police was because it was unusual for him to be home at that time of day. I wondered if he was off sick because there'd been a terrible bug going around.'

Seb nodded. 'Is that what you told the police? That Wes had been home all morning?'

'Yes.' Rosemary nodded, though colour rose up her cheeks. 'Well... no. At first I told them that I *thought* he might be home sick and would have been home all morning. Veronica had been poorly all week with the same bug, and I was very tired. I wasn't totally sure, but the officer said it was better to say I *had* seen his car there all morning, so that's what I did.'

'You then changed this statement, though. Why?' Birdie asked.

The older woman closed her eyes before answering. 'The police came back and explained that the postman had seen Wes driving to work so his car wasn't there the whole time. They asked if it was possible that I'd made a mistake and not seen Wes's car until later in the morning.'

'Which was the truth,' Veronica said. 'It was the police officer who told you to say the car was there all morning.'

'I know, but at the time I was tired and starting to feel sick. I ended up with the bug that you had. The detective was worried Wes would get away with killing Helen, and maybe go after someone else. I panicked, so changed my statement to what he said. I couldn't bear it if he went and killed someone else because of my evidence.'

'Oh, Mum.' Veronica let out a soft gasp and Birdie's stomach tightened with rage.

'Was the detective who told you to change your statement DC Jeff Dunbar?' Birdie asked.

'Maybe. I'm not sure. To be honest, I don't remember his name or what he looked like.'

'In DC Dunbar's notes he mentioned that you were on medication which made you a little woozy, is that correct?'

Rosemary frowned. 'I had taken some cold relief tablets. But I don't think they made me *woozy*.'

'Did you specifically tell the officer about the meds?' Birdie pushed.

'I'm sorry, I don't know.' Rosemary closed her eyes for a few seconds, as if trying to recollect.

'Is there a possibility that it wasn't Wes's car you saw during the morning?' Seb asked.

There was silence as Rosemary swallowed and began to shred the tissue in her hands.

'I'm sure there was a car. I suppose it might not have been his, but the police thought it was, and so I agreed. They said they were using my evidence to build their case. Is it because of my statement that you're looking into this for Daryl?'

'Not at all. All you were doing was assisting the police at a very difficult time.' Seb leant in closer to the older woman, his eyes solemn. 'No one is blaming you. There are many other things we're looking into that relate to the case. We appreciate you talking to us. You've been a huge help.'

Seb appeared to have the magic touch and Rosemary's panic subsided.

'That's very kind. Now, I think I'm ready for one of Veronica's cupcakes…'

Birdie and Seb stayed a further fifteen minutes before leaving, chatting to the older woman and making sure she was no longer distressed.

Veronica saw them out. 'Thank you for reassuring her. I had no idea what happened that day.'

'There was no way you could have unless your mum had mentioned it,' Birdie reminded her. 'Seb's right. This has helped a great deal. If your mum does remember anything else, please give us a call.'

'I will,' Veronica said and waited until they were at the bottom of the garden path before disappearing back into the house.

'Poor woman. I thought we were going to discover she had a grudge against Helen and Wes, but it sounds like Dunbar played upon her fears of being murdered in her own home,' Birdie said, once back in the car.

'I agree, and it throws up more questions than answers. Was Wes arrested because he was an easy target, or was it something else?'

Birdie twisted in her seat. 'Do you think Dunbar was bribed to pin it on Wes?'

'Possibly, or simply bribed to make sure TEC wasn't brought into it.'

'That makes sense, but my money's still on Roger North being involved,' Birdie said as Seb started the engine and headed back to the ring road. 'And before you say anything, I know we don't have any clear evidence... just call it a gut feeling.'

SEVENTEEN

Thursday, 24 July

'Does Roger North wear anything other than a DJ?' Birdie pushed back her desk chair and rolled it over to the French doors, where Elsa was standing, her nose pressed on the glass, wanting to go outside. 'It seems like all the photographs on his social media accounts are of him at some flashy charity event, sporting a black dinner jacket and bow tie. And how come he's so tanned in all of them? Don't tell me – skiing, tennis, and golf.'

'I expect he has a PR person whose job it is to promote him,' Seb replied, staring at one of the images Birdie had shown him of Roger North, who was tall and slim with silver hair.

'Well, they're doing a great job.' Birdie tickled Elsa's ears. 'According to his account, he still lives in Switzerland, but I can't find an address or phone number. I don't suppose your parents know him, by any chance? And before you say it, I know I ask that question when we come across anyone rich, but you never know.'

'As far as I'm aware, no, they don't.' Seb picked up his phone. 'I'll ask Rob if he can help,' he added, referring to his friend and ex-colleague DI Rob Lawson from the Metropolitan Police.

'Good idea. Send him my love and ask him to send more photos of Leo. That child's growing up so fast – I won't recognise him soon. I'll take Elsa outside for a quick walk while you chat.'

Birdie disappeared outside in a blur of energy, and Seb made the call.

'Clifford, to what do I owe this pleasure? It's good to know you haven't perished up there in the sticks.' Rob chuckled.

'I'm managing to survive as best I can. How are Maddie and Leo?'

'I last saw the pair of them buried under a pile of toys. How can a four-year-old kid need so many of them?' Rob complained, jokingly. 'You don't help. Each time you visit, you come loaded with presents.'

'How else can I retain my status as honorary uncle?'

'By babysitting,' Rob retorted, not missing a beat. 'Now, unless I'm mistaken, this isn't a social call. What's the problem?'

'We're working on a cold case and want to track down a property developer called Roger North. He was the managing director of Fullerton Construction, which went into receivership over twenty years ago. The firm was behind a large development in Leicester back in the late eighties, and it's our belief that they bribed their way through the planning process. He's been living in Switzerland ever since.'

'Your guy doesn't exactly sound like a choirboy if he headed straight to Switzerland.' Rob let out a snort of cynical laughter. 'I've never heard of him, but let me see what I can find out and get back to you. Before I go, how's my favourite partner of yours doing? You haven't scared her off yet?'

'Birdie's my only partner,' Seb retorted, intentionally appearing not to get the joke. 'But that aside, she's well and sends her love and is insisting on more photos of Leo.'

'Consider it done. And send mine back to her. Next time you visit, bring her, too.'

'Will do. Thanks.' Seb finished the call and stepped outside for a breath of fresh air. Birdie and Elsa were at the far end of the lawn, though Birdie was doing more running than Elsa, who was curled up, lazily pawing at a dandelion. He crossed over to join them.

'Well?' Birdie looked up, her cheeks bright from the exercise.

'Rob's agreed to look into it and get back to me.'

'That's great. Fingers crossed he can find something. Then again, I wouldn't complain about a trip to Switzerland to look for North.'

'That would be a tad on the expensive side but—' His phone rang.

Birdie grinned. 'Rob?'

'Yes.' Seb nodded and answered the call. 'That was quick. How did you go?'

'I found him in the records, so clearly he's on someone's radar. He's living in Cologny. It looks like he hasn't returned to the UK in five years.'

'Cologny? That place is exclusive.' Seb had visited the breath-taking town on the banks of Lake Geneva a couple of times and knew that if Roger North had retired there, he would have needed plenty of money.

'I'll take your word for it,' Rob said. 'I've emailed through an address and phone number to Birdie. I know that brain of yours won't forget it, but I'm guessing she's leaning over your shoulder, wanting to know what I've discovered.'

'Almost.' Seb bit back a smile as Birdie stood on her tiptoes to listen in on the call. 'I'll put you on speaker.'

'Hi, Birdie – I've sent you North's contact details and some photos of Leo,' Rob said.

'Thanks, Rob, you're a superstar.' Her phone pinged and

she answered it. 'Aww... look at the little scamp stuffing his face with chocolate cake.' She showed them to Seb. 'You know that kid is my guru.'

'It's not so funny when he makes a mess on my brother's white sofa. I'm still paying off the cleaning bill.' Rob laughed. 'We're not all loaded private investigators like you two.'

'If you ever decide to leave the force, let me know – we'd welcome you with open arms,' Seb said, knowing full well that his old friend would stay where he was until retirement. 'Before you go, could I ask one more favour?' Seb added. 'If North is being monitored, you'll know if he returns to the UK. Please could you let us know if he does?'

Rob was silent apart from the sound of rough scraping, suggesting he was rubbing his chin. Finally, he sighed. 'I take it you're only asking me because you and Birdie are in the process of stirring up trouble?'

'It's too early to say,' Seb admitted. 'But it's important to know North's whereabouts if we do discover that he's involved.'

'Fine. If his passport gets pinged coming through customs, I'll let you know. Now, I'd better go and make sure the wheels haven't fallen off my own case. Remember, both of you – watch out for this guy. The ones who hide in the shadows and have deep pockets are always the most dangerous, as you well know.'

'I told you I had a bad feeling about North,' Birdie said after Seb had ended the call. 'He could be a threat.'

'It's certainly something to be mindful of,' Seb agreed. 'We need to err on the side of caution.'

'Caution's my middle name,' Birdie assured him with a wink, then held out her phone. 'I've looked up North's address in Cologny. You weren't joking about it being exclusive. It looks like something from a James Bond set. Is that a helicopter pad on the roof?'

Seb shielded his eyes so he could see the screen. It was a

five-storey apartment block and North had one of the penthouses.

'It looks like it,' Seb said as they headed back to the office. 'I'll phone him now.' Seb settled into his chair and keyed in the number Rob had given him, before putting the phone onto speaker.

It rang three times before it was answered. 'Roger North speaking.'

'Mr North, my name's Sebastian Clifford. I'm a private investigator in the UK and we'd like to ask you a few questions about Tony Lucas.'

'I've never heard of the man,' North responded in clipped tones. 'Now, if you don't mind—'

'Actually, I do mind,' Seb cut in, equally sharp. 'The case we're working on involves your company, Fullerton Construction, and the building of Camberton Towers in Leicester. Our investigation is proving to be most enlightening.'

There was silence until they heard a low sigh. 'Who did you say you were?'

'Sebastian Clifford, and my partner, Birdie, is also here.'

In the background, Seb heard a murmur. Whoever was in the room with North had clearly done a name search on the internet. It appeared to be enough to stop the man from ending the call.

'I repeat, I've never heard that name before,' North said.

'I'll refresh your memory,' Seb said. 'Lucas worked as a town planner when your company was applying for permission to tear down Riddle Park in favour of your development. You were photographed together on at least one occasion. I can send you copies if that would help?'

'Oh, him,' North said, dismissively. 'You must forgive me for not remembering everyone's name. Especially on a project that happened so long ago. If I recall, the man was a social climber.

You'd be surprised how often people attempt to ride on one's coat tails, especially at social events. Is that all?'

'No. Our investigation has revealed that Lucas took bribes for pushing through planning applications. When permission for Camberton Towers was sought, there was considerable backlash against it, especially from the residents who lived on the estate and whose homes were to be demolished. Yet, it went through relatively easily.'

'Are you saying that I bribed a council official?' North's voice was brittle.

'Did you?' Seb pushed.

'I did not,' the man retorted. 'I pride myself on integrity and honesty. If you're suggesting that Lucas was corrupt, you'll have to take it up with him.'

'Lucas is dead.'

'Is he now?' North let out a bark of laughter. 'Then it seems to me all you're doing is fishing. Let me give you a friendly warning: don't waste your time trying to accuse me of something you can't substantiate. I'm a well-respected businessman with *many* friends.'

'I'm sure you are,' Seb agreed. 'The problem with having so many friends is that some of them might want to talk. Like Maurice Bryant, for example. Was he one of your *friends*?'

'I've never heard of him,' North snapped back, his words once again clipped. 'Let me guess, you have a photograph of us together as well?'

'Not yet. Do you think we'll find one?' Seb countered.

This time, the silence lasted even longer. 'What's this really about?' North finally demanded.

'We're investigating the murder of a thirty-seven-year-old woman called Helen Brackstone. She was a member of a group who were unhappy with the development and she, in particular, spent time investigating it. She was poisoned in her own home and her husband was convicted of her murder. He died in jail.'

'I have no idea what you're talking about. This call is over. If I hear from you again, I will be instructing my lawyer. Are we clear, Mr Clifford?'

Without another beat, the line went dead.

Birdie was immediately up on her feet and began to pace. 'Well, he certainly didn't let me down. Did you believe a word he said?'

'No. But I do believe he thinks he can fix everything using threats and intimidation. The fact he refused to answer any questions makes it more likely that he knew exactly who Tony Lucas, Maurice Bryant, and Helen Brackstone were.'

'We'll have to find another way to prove his involvement. I'll start looking for other links.'

Seb nodded, as he returned to his attention to the computer. Rob was right. They were shaking things up, which meant they were moving in the right direction.

EIGHTEEN

Friday, 25 July

'What do you think? Is it too much?' Keira spun around to show off the blue floral-print skirt with ruffles that she was wearing. Then she wrinkled her nose and let out a small wail. 'Of course it's too much. I'll change back into my jeans.'

'You've already changed three times.' Birdie picked up an apple from the kitchen bench and polished it like a cricket ball. Seb had mentioned yesterday that he and Keira were meeting Dr Georgina 'George' Cavendish for lunch, but Birdie hadn't expected the nineteen-year-old to be so wound up about her appearance – especially when she looked like a supermodel in everything she wore. *Long legs are wasted on the tall*, Birdie mused to herself. 'Why are you freaking out?' she said out loud. 'The skirt's great. Look how sunny it is. If you wear jeans, your legs will be sticking together before you even arrive there.'

'Good point.' Keira took a deep breath and sat down at the kitchen table. 'I'm so nervous about meeting George again. You know how elegant she is. I don't want her to think I'm wasting her time.'

'I've seen you hold your own with Seb's entire family, and they're a whole different level. Not to mention you killed your first-year exams. If anything, George will respect you for looking into various options so thoroughly. Is something else going on?'

Keira was silent as she studied her nail polish, but when she looked up, the panic in her eyes had faded.

'It's nerves, that's all. Sorry for all the drama.'

'What drama?' Seb asked as he walked into the kitchen. He stared at his daughter. 'You've changed again?'

'It's too hot for jeans, so I decided on a skirt,' Keira said with a flick of her chin, sounding more like her usual self.

Which was good. Birdie had come to think of Keira as a little sister and didn't like seeing her off-kilter. She took a bite of the apple and joined them at the kitchen table.

'So, while you two are stuffing your faces with lobster, I'll be here, single-handedly looking after the office.'

'Lobster? Eww.' Keira pulled a face. 'No, thank you.'

'I might refrain as well,' Seb said, though a smile twitched at his lips. 'By the way, how did you get on last night?'

The previous afternoon, she'd spent time trying to track down Roger North's secretary – who'd moved to New Zealand – and she worked late attempting to contact the woman.

'It was a dead end,' Birdie said, sighing. 'She'd moved. No forwarding address. How about you?'

'Not much better. North is the master of shielding behind shell companies. I'll continue this afternoon.'

'I don't have great news either,' Keira added. 'I found application numbers for five of Fullerton's projects, including Camberton Towers. But none of the applications are available online. They've been archived, so we can either put in a request, which might take a few days, or view them in person at the council offices. Shall we head there after lunch, Dad?'

'I've got a better idea,' Birdie said, jumping to her feet. 'I'll go there now. It'll be nice to get out of the office, and then we can work on them together once you're back from lunch.'

'That's fine with me,' Seb said, nodding.

Keira's phone beeped. 'Dad, that's my alarm. We need to go now.'

'It's only ten-thirty. We're not due there until twelve,' Seb reminded her, but Keira was already heading for the door.

'Yes, but what if we get stuck behind a tractor? Or there's a traffic jam on the motorway? It's better to be early,' she lectured, her voice fading as she disappeared into the hallway.

Birdie raised an eyebrow. 'I've never seen her so excited before.'

'I agree. But if she does want to become a forensic psychologist, then George is an excellent role model.'

Seb retrieved his keys, and they both followed Keira outside. Birdie waited until Seb's BMW had disappeared from view before climbing into her own car. The sun had reappeared from behind a bank of clouds as the low hedges and green fields flashed past. It was perfect cricketing weather, and she hoped it would continue for tomorrow afternoon's match. It was against one of their local rivals and should be a good game.

Melinda was going to be there. Birdie pulled out her phone and read through their text messages from the previous evening.

> Hey Melinda. Just checking you're still coming to the match. First ball's at 2pm 🏏

> > Definitely! Even if I still don't understand the game. Should I bring anything?

> Yourself, and maybe a camping chair if you've got one. Matches can last a few hours. I'll explain what's happening between overs 😊

> > Haha. I'm counting on it. And thanks for the tip about the chair. I'll pack some snacks for us if you like?

> That would be amazing. I always get hungry after batting. Looking forward to seeing you there.

> Me too. I'll be the one cheering way too loudly when you score... What's it called again? A run 😳

Even though they got on so well, Birdie still hadn't given an answer about the date. Her heart was telling her to say yes, but her head was telling her otherwise. Work was full on and committing to a relationship could be problematic; either Birdie would end up cancelling dates, or – worse – becoming so distracted that she couldn't do her job properly.

Or was she overthinking?

It wouldn't be the first time.

She started the engine and headed down the drive, turning in the direction of Leicester. After a few miles, a cyclist drifted across the narrow country lane and Birdie braked. She checked her rear-view mirror at a white Ford Ranger behind her. Instead of slowing down, it flashed its lights, as if it was her fault.

Irritation crawled along her skin. If she'd still been on the force, she'd have flagged him down and informed him that tailgating was illegal. As it was, she turned her attention back to the cyclist, who stayed in the middle of the road for a quarter of a mile, before finally turning into a farm entrance where there was a small produce stand selling strawberries.

Hoooooonk.

The sharp blast of a car horn rang out, and once again, she checked the mirror. It was the Ford again. She gritted her teeth, but didn't increase her speed. It seemed to work, and they backed off. If they were in such a hurry to get past her, why didn't they overtake? The road was straight and clear. There was no one behind the Ford, either. They seriously should calm down, because...

Hoooooonk.

What the…? Her fingers tightened around the steering wheel as the vehicle loomed large in the mirror. There was only one occupant in the car. A man in a black jacket, his face half hidden under a cap. Was he trying to piss her off? If so, congratulations. It was working.

The sun glinted off the dazzling white paintwork and the driver suddenly flicked on his full beam. She stiffened her shoulders, but kept her speed at the legal limit. The horn blared out for a third time, and her heart hammered in her chest. She'd just about had enough of this.

She twisted her neck to study the driver, only to be met with the roar of the engine and squeal of tyres as the vehicle crossed over the broken white line. But instead of passing her, it pulled up alongside her, so close they were almost touching.

Hooooooonk. Hooooooonk. Hooooonk.

Adrenaline flooded her system as the hulking vehicle pressed closer to her car. Birdie gritted her teeth and spun the steering wheel, desperate to find some space. But the narrow A-road was lined with hedges, making it impossible to go anywhere.

What the hell?

Still, the Ford moved her closer into the side of the road until branches from the hedge scraped along the left-hand side of her car. Her tyres bounced over a low ditch, and she slammed on her brakes, bringing the car to a halt. Her seatbelt snapped tightly against her body and her heart pounded in her ears as she tried to catch her breath. Her chest was tight, and she turned towards the Ford, but it suddenly revved its engine and roared away.

Birdie's shock was replaced with fury, and years of habit tuned her scattered wits to narrow in on the number plate. She repeated it twice, while at the same time snatching her phone from the passenger seat, taking several photos before the vehicle was too far away.

She leant back in the seat and waited for the drum-like beat of her heart to quieten down. Her hands were still shaking, but she focused on her breathing, knowing it was the fastest way to calm down. *In. Out. In. Out. In. Out.*

This wasn't just an impatient driver. This was something else entirely.

Birdie pulled up the photograph on her phone to make sure she'd captured the number plate. It was clear as day and meant she could find out who the car belonged to. Why would someone do this? Was it just random, or... her stomach clenched... could it be connected to the case?

She couldn't leave without assessing the damage, though, and her jaw clenched at the thought of what she might find. Shoving her car door open, she stormed around to the passenger side. The sight made her blood boil. Ugly scratches across the door and above the front tyre. The new car was her pride and joy, and she didn't need this.

She dragged in a couple of deep breaths, trying to shake off her annoyance, but her calming routine was interrupted by her phone pinging with a text message. It wasn't a number she recognised, and she tapped the screen.

> Drop the Brackstone case or you won't be so lucky next time.

Birdie stared at it for several seconds as the realisation of what it meant hit her hard.

She'd been run off the road intentionally.

It was a warning.

Anger coursed through her.

Was Roger North behind it?

She'd bet he was. Seb had said yesterday that the man thought he could fix everything by threats and intimidation.

He should have done nothing. Because now they had proof there was more to Helen's murder than first thought.

'And I'm going to find out what it is,' Birdie muttered to herself as she climbed back into the driver's seat and toyed with her phone.

Her first instinct was to call Seb, but if she did, he might insist on returning straight away and she knew how much Keira wanted to meet up with George.

Now that the adrenaline had lessened, she began to work it all out. Had North paid someone to watch them at the office? If so, had they guessed where she was going? Were they trying to stop her from visiting the planning office?

Well, that wasn't going to stop her. She would definitely go. But before she did, she wanted to discover the driver's name and if he was linked to North.

She scrolled through her phone and made a call.

'Birdie, what's up?' Twiggy answered on the fourth ring; in the background, she could hear a rowdy conversation going on. Twiggy muttered something under his breath. 'Hang on a minute. I'm going outside. A man can't hear himself think in this place.'

'No probs,' Birdie said.

'That's better,' Twiggy said after a little while. 'How can I help?'

'Can you do me a favour and run a plate for me, please?'

'Why? What's happened? Is this about the Brackstone case?' Twiggy responded.

Birdie sucked in a breath. Twiggy would be just as likely as Seb to drop everything and start fussing over her if she told him what happened. More importantly, he would tell her to go home – and turn the whole case over to the police.

'Relax. Nothing's happened.' She crossed her fingers. 'You're right about it being about Helen's murder. I think the owner of a white Ford Ranger has some information we need.'

'Why didn't you call in to see me?' Twiggy demanded, clearly still suspicious.

Birdie gritted her teeth. Over the years, people had underestimated Twiggy because of his laid-back attitude and scruffy appearance, but underneath, he'd always been shrewd. Even with his frontotemporal dementia diagnosis, that hadn't changed. Well, not yet.

'I'm not in Market Harborough,' she retorted. 'Please, Twig. I wouldn't ask if it wasn't important.'

'Yeah, yeah, I know,' he relented. 'Give me the number and I'll check. I'll call you back with the details, but it might be a while – there's a meeting starting in ten minutes to do some new regulations – borrr-ing...'

A loud pretend yawn came down the phone, and she laughed.

'I'm sure you'll enjoy it. Thanks. You're a lifesaver.'

After ending the call, Birdie started the engine and continued driving. The rest of the journey to Leicester was uneventful, and it wasn't long before she was waiting in a queue at the reception counter of the planning office. It was almost lunchtime and there were several people in front of her. Finally, she reached the front.

'Sorry about the wait. How can I help?' a friendly man asked.

He appeared to be her age, which meant he wouldn't have known Tony Lucas or Maurice Bryant from their time in the office.

'I'd like to take a look at some planning applications from the 1980s. I have the number for each one.' Birdie gave him the details Keira had texted, half expecting him to refuse, but instead, he jotted them down and asked her to take a seat.

He returned twenty minutes later with a pile of folders and took her through to a small booth with a table and chair.

'You're in luck. We've still got the original files for the

applications you're interested in. Most of our older files are only accessible on microfiche because of storage issues. You're welcome to look at them here, but if you'd like any copies, there's a charge.'

'I understand. Thank you.'

Birdie took the files from him and sat at the table. After the morning she'd had, it was good to be able to focus on something. She was more motivated than ever to discover how closely North and Lucas were connected and if it could be tied back to their case.

NINETEEN

Friday, 25 July

'Yes.' Birdie stood up from behind her office desk and punched the air.

She'd started going through the files at the planning office, but her eyes had glazed over after a few minutes, so she'd ended up taking photos of all the documents. After driving home and having a quick lunch, she began going through them more carefully.

And there it was.

Tony Lucas's scrawling signature of approval at the bottom of the documents for all five applications that North's company had submitted to Leicester City Council planning department in the 1980s.

In each case, the developments had gone ahead, despite there being a wave of public disapproval, which appeared to have been ignored.

No wonder Helen had been so determined to expose them.

Birdie shuddered at the memory of the Ford Ranger trying to run her off the road. If North, or whoever else was involved, felt it necessary to have her followed thirty-six years later, it wasn't a stretch of the imagination to assume they'd done the same, and worse, to Helen and Maurice Bryant.

Her phone rang, and Twiggy's name flashed up on the screen.

'Twig, how did you get on?' she asked, without even saying hello.

'That's a matter of opinion,' he retorted, his voice tight. 'The owner of the car is Joseph Pike and, before you ask, I did look him up. He's not the sort of man who'd stop to let little old ladies cross the road.'

'I take it he's got a record?'

'As long as my arm, and then some,' Twiggy replied, letting out a long sigh. 'He's sixty-six and has been in and out of jail for years. Currently, he's out on parole. He's extremely violent and if he's connected to the Brackstone case, Birdie, you'd better be careful. And I'm not joking.'

'I will, don't worry,' she promised. 'Do you have a photo and an address?'

'Not if you're going to visit him alone,' Twiggy said flatly.

'I'll go with Seb as soon as he gets back'

'In that case, I'll text them to him.'

'You can't do that because he doesn't know anything about it yet. I promise not to go alone. Trust me.'

'You'd better not be lying.'

'I'm not. You know me better than that.'

'Hmm. That's what I'm worried about.' He paused for a second. 'Okay then. But I'm warning you...' His words fell away, but their meaning hung in the air.

Her phone pinged within a few seconds. 'Thanks, Twig. You're the best.'

'Yeah, and a fat lot of good it's ever done me,' he grumbled, but Birdie could tell he was smiling. 'Clear off then – I've got better things to do than talk to you all afternoon.'

'Of course you do... We'll go out for a drink soon. My shout.'

'Now that I'd like to see,' he said as they ended the call.

Birdie opened a new tab on her computer and keyed in Joseph Pike's name. Despite having no access to police records, she got plenty of results. Most were from newspaper articles, but she did find a couple of social media accounts, neither of which were set to private.

She went through the first one, but there weren't many posts, and most of the friends appeared to be fake accounts. She went deeper into those who appeared genuine. One of them led her to several photos of Joseph Pike over the years, mainly at a pub or racecourse. It wasn't much, but it helped her build a basic profile and she collated it in a folder.

The sound of tyres on the drive distracted her.

Seb and Keira were back.

She closed the screen and walked out to meet them. Keira bounced out of the car, almost before Seb had turned off the engine. Her cheeks were glowing and her eyes bright. Birdie suppressed a smile. Clearly, all the worrying about what to wear was a thing of the past.

'I hope it wasn't too boring?' she teased, and Keira burst out laughing as Seb joined them.

'You're hilarious. In case you couldn't guess, it was sooooo good. Whitney was there as well, and was telling me all about their most recent cases. Then George talked me through what my options would be if I transferred and what kind of career I could have. Plus, she took me around Lenchester University, including the library. I can already see myself going there. I'm going upstairs to my room to call my friend Lucy. She'll be dying to know how it went.'

Once Keira had disappeared into the house, Birdie turned to Seb and studied his face. How was he taking it? She knew he'd been worried about Keira changing courses.

'I take it George was okay with the idea?'

'Yes, she approved,' he admitted as they walked back inside. 'Whitney's daughter, Tiffany, studied at Lenchester. Whitney also asked how I found raising a child as a solo parent, because she'd done it.'

'In front of Keira?' Birdie asked, frowning.

'No, it was after lunch in one of the university cafés. George took Keira on a short tour leaving us alone for a while. It was good to compare her experience with mine.'

'And remember, Whitney did it all while climbing the ladder as a detective,' she said.

Birdie had long respected DCI Walker and still considered the woman a role model.

'Indeed,' Seb agreed as they reached the office. 'How did your visit to the planning office go, and what happened to the car? I saw the scratches.'

'Trust you to notice.' She closed the door behind them. 'Don't worry, I was going to tell you but didn't want to worry Keira.'

His brows furrowed and concern shone from his eyes. 'Are you okay?'

'I'm fine. But no thanks to the car that tried to run me off Farndon Road earlier.'

She explained what had happened and showed him the text.

After reading it, he strode over to the window and stared outside.

'Why didn't you call me?' Seb asked as he turned back to face her, his mouth pinched.

'Because there was nothing you could do about it, and I didn't want to interfere with the lunch.' Birdie nodded towards the ceiling in the direction of Keira's bedroom. 'I asked Twiggy to run the plates and he called me back with a name – Joseph Pike – and an address. He's currently on parole.'

'I take it you didn't tell him *why* you wanted the information?'

Birdie sighed. 'I can't get anything past you. No, I didn't tell him, because you know what he's like. He'd go all protective over me and I don't need it.'

'In this instance, he'd have been entirely justified. If this man was prepared to run you off the road in his own vehicle while on parole, it means he's either being paid extremely well, or he's lacking in intelligence. I suspect it's the former.'

'Or it could even be both. From my research, I've discovered he's a known associate of several high-profile gang bosses. Although it seems he's near the bottom of the pecking order.'

'That makes him dangerous. If he's managed to stay alive this long, we can't underestimate him.'

'Totally. You do realise that if North's behind this, we must have rattled him.'

'Which means we need to be very careful from now on. Were you followed on your way to the planning office?'

'No. Pike drove off and I didn't see him again. Oh, before I forget, I've sent you photographs of the five planning applications that Fullerton Construction made. They were all rubber stamped by Lucas, which does bring everything back to North, yet again.'

'All the more reason to tread carefully with Pike,' Seb acknowledged while walking over to the desk and sitting down.

Birdie sat opposite him. 'I've been thinking about how to approach Pike. Rather than go in all guns blazing, we should put him under surveillance and see where it leads us.'

Her answer seemed to appease him, and his shoulders relaxed. 'That's a good idea. We'll start tomorrow.'

'Sorry, I have a match,' Birdie explained. 'But that aside, let's wait until Monday, in case he's still watching me. We can lull him into thinking that his threats have worked because I'm not working on the case and we're just having a normal weekend.'

'Yes, I agree that's the best course of action. Although, I'm concerned about how Pike knows you,' Seb said, rubbing his chin. 'We're assuming that North sent him, but we only spoke to him yesterday. Pike could have been instructed by Black, although I doubt he'd have the money to pay him, or he's been involved from the start.'

'Crap – that means...' Birdie's words fell away.

She'd been so focused on Pike and her visit to the planning office that she hadn't considered that Seb might have been followed, too. By not calling and warning him, he and Keira could have been in danger.

Her dismay must have shone through on her face because Seb shook his head. 'I know how to spot a tail and we weren't followed to Lenchester.'

'All the same, next time I promise to call you immediately.'

'I have no doubt,' he agreed. 'It's in your DNA to never make the same mistake twice – apart from with timekeeping,' he said with a smile, clearly trying to pacify her, which she appreciated.

'That's different – some things are hardwired.' She grinned.

'We need to know why they decided to follow you and not me? Had they been watching the office?' Seb mused.

'Impossible,' Birdie retorted, getting to her feet. 'They'd have to be up a tree with binoculars, or using a drone, because there's no way they can easily hide along the road outside this place, and it's not like any of the neighbours would have tipped them off.'

'There is one other way.' Seb opened a drawer in the desk and pulled out a long-handled mirror and a torch.

He strode out the French doors, across the grass and round to the front of the house where both the cars were parked.

'You're thinking a tracking device?' Birdie asked, jogging to keep up with him.

'They're inexpensive and one doesn't need to be a criminal mastermind to use them.'

His mouth was set in a grim line as he reached her beloved new car and lowered himself to the ground. Using the mirror, beginning at the wheel hubs, he slowly moved his way along, looking more like a dentist than a detective.

'This is so bloody annoying,' she muttered as he continued his search.

'If I don't locate one, the next step is to purchase a sweeper, although it will only work when the engine's running—' He broke off. 'Look, there it is.'

She crouched down and craned her neck until she could see the small black box that had been attached to the inside of the hub. Irritation surged through her at the idea someone had purposely put it there.

'Is it attached by a magnet?' She stretched out her arm to reach for it, but Seb stopped her.

'Pike will know if you do that, and for now it's best if we don't give him any reason to think we're onto him. Let me check my car,' Seb said, standing and heading over to his black BMW.

Seb repeated the sweep on his own vehicle before finally stepping away. 'It appears that my car's clean. It's possible the tracking device on yours was attached while you were parked outside your parents' house in Market Harborough.'

'That means Pike or someone else was skulking outside and followed me home. Somehow, that seems even worse than running me off the road.'

She clenched her fists, still fighting the urge to rip the tracker away.

'Yes, I believe you're right. If I thought it would help, I'd confront Pike now. But we should play it safe, or more people might be at risk. I suspect the only reason there isn't a device on my car is because Pike couldn't simply stroll up the drive, as he'd have been seen.'

'Now I need to add "long, gated driveway" to my house search,' Birdie retorted and then rolled her shoulders. 'Sorry, I'm so angry.'

'Understandable,' Seb said, his jaw tight. 'But now we know the type of people we're up against. I suggest we keep the tracker on your car but hire a different vehicle when we begin our surveillance on Monday. Even without a tracker on my car, it's distinctive and he might have seen it. There's also Daryl's safety to consider. If Black's involved, he might have mentioned her to North or Pike.'

Birdie closed her eyes. The ripple effect of North's threat was reaching further than she'd first thought.

'Do you think they'll go after her, like they did with her mother?'

'I hope not, but it's not a risk we can take. We'll visit her now and check her car. Then we'll discuss options. I'll call her.' Seb pulled out his phone and made the call.

'She's planning to visit her daughter soon. Why don't we encourage her to go now and stay there until the investigation's over,' Birdie suggested, once he'd finished talking with Daryl.

'That's an excellent idea. Daryl's at home now and, as you heard, I said we'd be there in half an hour. I suggest you drive back to your house, and I'll collect you from there in a taxi. This weekend, you must be vigilant and keep me updated on where you are and where you're intending to go.'

Birdie reluctantly nodded. She was private by nature, but Seb was right. While the tracker was on the car, she'd have to be careful.

TWENTY

Monday, 28 July

Joseph Pike lived in a small 1970s terraced house with a large BEWARE OF THE DOG sign in the front window. Seb had parked the hire car several doors down from the house, but in the last hour, there had been no signs of life from the property.

'Clearly he's not a morning person,' Birdie said from next to him. She had a cricket cap pulled over her red curls and was tapping her foot against the floor of the gun-metal-grey Renault they'd hired for the week. 'Where's his car? It's definitely not anywhere round here.'

'Maybe it's parked in a garage elsewhere to prevent people from seeing him driving it?' Seb suggested.

'Yeah, or he doesn't want to risk some low life putting a tracker on it,' Birdie muttered. 'Not that I'm calling us *low life*, or implying that we'd put a tracker on his car – although maybe we should, what do you think?'

'It's illegal, as you well know.'

'True...' Birdie said with a resigned sigh.

'I take it you didn't see him watching you over the weekend?' Seb asked, steering the conversation away from potential lawbreaking.

'No, luckily for him. If he'd been around, I'd have been tempted to run *him* off the road,' she retorted, then held up her hands. 'Not that I would have... I don't think. Anyway, thanks to him, I was so wound up and frustrated that I had a killer innings, hitting three sixes in a row.'

'It's good to know you were able to channel your rage,' Seb replied, repressing a smile.

'What about you? How was your weekend?' Birdie asked.

He didn't want to let on that he'd spent an uncomfortable couple of days worried that Pike might approach Birdie, or go near Daryl. Although Daryl had taken the news calmly, and had been relieved when there was no sign of a tracker on her car, she'd agreed to catch the train to Dorset that same afternoon. Seb and Birdie had driven Daryl to the station, and she'd checked in with him several times over the weekend.

One less thing to worry about.

'It was good,' he simply answered. 'Sorry I didn't make it to the match. Sarah's twins came for a visit and we had lunch together.'

Birdie had met his cousin's sons several times over the years and tended to think of them much like she did her own younger brothers.

'How are they doing now they've graduated?' Birdie asked.

'Benedict's starting a job in London next month, and Caspian's heading to Thailand to meet up with his mother and— Look,' Seb said, pointing to the front door of Pike's house.

The door had opened, and out of the darkness stepped Joseph Pike. He might have been sixty-six, but his body was well toned, and he had the stance of a boxer. His grey hair was long and oiled back over his ears and an ankle monitor was visible below his black jeans and sage-green polo shirt.

Seb and Birdie slipped down in their seats, but Pike didn't

even glance in their direction as he fished a phone from his pocket and made a call. He walked in the opposite direction from where they were parked and turned left.

'Come on, let's follow him,' Birdie said, jumping out of the car.

Seb did the same and they hurried down the street, keeping Pike at a distance until finally he reached a scruffy-looking café next to a betting shop and walked inside.

'Let's stand over there.' Birdie pointed to a shop doorway which gave them a good view of the café. It was easy to see Pike, who'd settled into a window seat.

'He's certainly not worried about being seen.'

'That's most obliging of him,' Birdie muttered. 'Though I still don't trust myself near him, in case I accidentally run a coin down his car as payback. Except we don't yet know where his car is.'

'I hope you didn't dwell on the tracker all weekend?' Seb turned to her, and she reluctantly smiled.

'Maybe not *all* weekend,' she admitted before nodding in the direction of the café window. 'Look, someone's just tapped on the window where Pike's sitting.'

Seb followed her gaze as a young man in a grey hoodie walked into the café and straight over to Pike, had a brief conversation, then headed back outside.

Pike then took a phone call and sat with a mug in front of him, which he occasionally sipped from. At twelve noon, he was joined by another man.

'Someone needs to tell that guy he's overdressed. He'd be more at home at a wine bar than in there,' Birdie said.

Seb agreed. The man looked a little younger than Pike and was wearing a well-cut navy suit, crisp white shirt and plain tie, all of which appeared bespoke, even from that distance. It was in stark contrast to Pike's well-worn polo shirt and jeans.

The two men leant in slightly, deep in conversation.

'It certainly doesn't look like a social get-together,' Seb said.

'My guess is that he's either hired Pike before, or is doing so now.'

Birdie pulled out her phone and took several photographs of them. The men remained conversing for ten minutes before the well-dressed man left.

'This looks promising. I'll follow him,' Seb said, pulling his jacket around him and getting ready to take off.

'Don't turn off your phone so we can track each other. If Pike stirs, I'll send you a text and follow him, too.'

Seb waited until the man had gone a little way and then crossed the road. The man didn't seem to be in a hurry as he strolled down the street. Seb had no problem keeping him in sight although he had to be careful not to get too close.

The man slowed down outside the entrance to a stationer's and stepped inside. Seb came to a halt, pretending to study his phone. While it would have been safer to wait outside, Seb couldn't risk there being a second entrance through which the man might disappear.

Decision made, he sent Birdie a quick text with an update and then walked into the shop.

The man was leaning over a display cabinet, studying the fountain pens. Seb hovered near a rack of greeting cards, while the man purchased the pen along with a copy of the *Financial Times*, after which he walked to the rear of the shop and outside.

Seb let out a breath. He'd made the right call.

Keeping an even pace, Seb trailed behind him, until he reached a small side street lined with uninspiring four- and five-storey brick office buildings.

The man walked into the first building on the left, crossed the foyer towards the lift, and stepped inside once the door had slid open. Seb didn't want to risk drawing attention to himself by following so, instead, he moved out of the way while staring at his phone. The lift door closed without anyone else entering, and Seb checked the progress on the digital display. It climbed to the fourth level and came to a halt. Seb pressed the button to call it back down and then took a step to the side.

The lift didn't stop on its way down and when the doors opened, it was empty. This confirmed that the man had alighted at the fourth floor. There was a large wall directory on the other side of the foyer.

There were three businesses on that level: EcoCleaners, GM Group – a recruitment consultancy – and Thornton & Rice, a firm of solicitors.

The hairs on the back of Seb's neck prickled. He'd spent yesterday afternoon going through the planning applications that Birdie had copied on Friday, and each application had listed Thornton & Rice as acting solicitor for Fullerton Construction.

Seb had already planned to investigate the solicitors' once they'd returned to the office, but now it was a priority. Using his phone, he googled Thornton & Rice and in less than ten seconds, he was staring at their smart navy-and-gold website.

The firm specialised in conveyancing, and there were several photos of the two partners. One of whom was William Thornton, the man he'd been pursuing. The company had been set up by the man's father, and William had joined in 1985.

Pocketing his phone, Seb retraced his steps. He walked past Norm's Café and noted that Pike was still seated at the table.

'Pike hasn't moved since you left,' Birdie complained once he'd reached her, still standing in the shop doorway. 'I hope you have news.'

'I do. Pike met with solicitor William Thornton, whose office is a fifteen-minute walk from here. Thornton and Rice were the solicitors on record for the planning applications you gave me.'

'Fantastic. We now have enough to *chat* with Pike, and there's no time like the present.'

TWENTY-ONE

Monday, 28 July

Norm's Café was made up of a large square room with mock wooden panelling on the walls and rows of white laminated tables and plastic chairs, which suggested it hadn't been updated since the sixties. Despite the grim décor, the place was full, with tradespeople and office workers alike, all tucking into their meals. The bustle of the kitchen was interspersed with the low buzz of conversation.

The counter was at the back of the café, and there was a long queue, so Seb and Birdie didn't bother pretending to be customers. Instead, they headed straight to Pike's table. His head was bowed over his phone, allowing Birdie to slip in opposite him while Seb sat next to him, effectively blocking him from leaving.

'Piss off, these seats are taken,' Pike growled, glancing up at them, his mouth set in an angry line. When neither of them moved, he put down his phone and let his gaze bounce between them. 'Who the hell are you?'

'Should I be hurt that you don't recognise me?' Birdie took

off the cap holding her red curls in place. They sprang out around her face.

'Sorry, love, I prefer blondes,' Pike growled, his mouth twitching as he quickly snatched up his phone and pocketed it.

Was he planning to make a run for it?

Seb leant in closer to him to dispel him of the notion.

'That's okay. You're not my type either,' Birdie assured him. 'Being on parole and all that. Speaking of which, I'll need to contact your parole officer to ask them to check your whereabouts last Friday at twelve thirty-five in the afternoon.'

'I don't know what you're talking about.' Pike's jaw flexed. He clearly had a short fuse.

'Let me jog your memory. You were heading north on the Farndon Road and ran my car off the road into a hedge. Did you forget about the ankle monitor you're wearing?' Birdie asked, holding Pike's mutinous glare. 'Surely you didn't believe your stupid tactic would scare me off?'

'Word to the wise,' Seb said, pressing his shoulder against Pike. 'My partner doesn't scare that easily.'

The man scowled and slumped back in his seat. 'What do you want?'

'Did you also send a threatening text, telling me to drop the case looking into the murder of Helen Brackstone?' Birdie asked, coldly.

'No. You can look for yourself.' He pulled out his phone.

'The message came in five minutes after you ran me off the road. So, either you sent it, or you had a second person assisting. We can always dig deeper and contact all your associates... We'll tell them that Pike sent us.'

Irritation crossed his face. 'Good luck with that. Most of them are either in the nick or lying in a hospital bed.'

'Seems your lifestyle isn't a very healthy one,' Seb commented. 'Back to the question. Did you send the threatening text?'

'Why would I? I've never even heard of the bird. Now, if that's—'

'That *bird* has a name. Helen Brackstone. She was murdered,' Birdie snapped, her hands clenched into fists. The casual dismissal of Helen's life hit a nerve.

'Whoever paid you to deliver the warning is tied up in it. We're not leaving until you tell us what you know.' Seb shifted in the chair until he was facing Pike.

'You can't prove nothing.' The man gave him a sullen glare.

'Really? I suppose that means you remembered to wear gloves when you put the tracker on my car and avoided the security cameras outside the houses in our street?' Birdie's annoyance had morphed into a glacial smile, and after several seconds of silence, Pike dropped his shoulders.

'Fine. You're right. I sent the text using a burner.'

'Did you fit the tracking device, too?' Seb asked.

'Yes. That was me. I was planning to do the black BMW as well.' He finally met Seb's gaze. 'Yours, I suppose. But so far it's been impossible to get to. It's much easier when a car's parked on the street all night.'

'Who paid you?' Birdie demanded.

'You know I can't tell you that.' Pike rolled his eyes.

'You can't afford *not* to,' Birdie retorted, pointing at Pike's ankle monitor. 'How's this going to look on your parole record?'

'Look, I couldn't tell you, even if I wanted to – the guy never gave me his name. That's how these things work.'

'Yeah, pull the other one,' Birdie snapped. 'No way would you take a job that could land you back in jail, unless they paid you so much you were prepared to take the risk.'

'Now you know,' Pike said with a shrug.

'Why did William Thornton pay you to threaten my colleague?' Seb cut in.

The blunt question appeared to catch Pike off guard, and

surprise flickered in his eyes. He gave Seb a murderous stare, then swore under his breath.

'Why are you asking if you already know?' Pike muttered.

'We wanted to hear it from you,' Seb said.

'How long have you been watching me?' Pike asked.

'Long enough to see your meeting with Thornton,' Birdie said, leaning in slightly. 'How do you know him?'

'If I tell you everything, then you better keep me out of this. Don't tell my parole officer.'

Seb and Birdie exchanged a glance.

'It depends on what you tell us,' Birdie said.

Pike sighed and rubbed his chin. 'Okay. I've known Thornton for years. We first met in the eighties. I'd just got out of jail and got a message that some flash git needed a hand with a job. It was going to be easy money.'

'What was this "job"?' Seb asked.

'Thornton had a client who ran a cleaning company – and before you ask, no, I can't remember the name. This chap was being sued by someone and Thornton paid me to *encourage* that someone to drop the case.'

'Did they?' Birdie asked, her mouth twitching with dislike.

'Yeah,' Pike responded, smirking. 'A few slaps is all it took.'

'I take it this led to further arrangements between the two of you?' Seb asked.

'Correct. Sometimes I'd pay people a visit and do over their place a bit. Or do over them. Thornton was more interested in results rather than methods. Like I said, it was easy money.'

'How often did he hire you to scare people off?' Birdie wanted to know.

'Enough to keep me in beer. But that was a long time ago. I'm a reformed character now.'

'Clearly not considering what happened on the Friday...' Birdie fixed him with a cold stare. 'What were your instructions?'

'I was given your details and told to stop you from investigating the case.'

'Did Thornton tell you to put trackers on the cars?' Birdie asked.

'No. I did it to keep an eye on you. To make sure you obeyed. Thornton left the details to me.' Pike shifted his gaze to check the café, as if he wanted to see if they were being watched. Then he inched forward. 'Thornton might dress all fancy, but he represents some real shady people who you don't want to get on the wrong side of.'

'Including Roger North?' Seb asked with a cool smile. Pike's back stiffened and he looked down. 'How often did you warn off people who got in Roger North's way?'

Pike let out a bitter laugh. 'It didn't work like that. I wasn't told *why* someone was being warned off. I was just given the message and delivered it. I was the guy in the middle.'

'Try again,' Birdie said, rolling her eyes, 'because you're talking crap. What jobs did you do for Roger North and how well did you know him?'

Pike held up both hands. 'I never met North, and that's the truth. But I knew the risk for anyone who got in his way – he had a habit of wanting his problems to disappear permanently, if you get what I mean?'

'He paid you to kill people?' Birdie's eyes flashed as she ground out the words.

'Not me, no way – that's not my style. But that was the word on the street.'

'What did you and Thornton discuss earlier?' Seb asked, bringing the conversation back to the meeting.

'I told him everything went as expected and there shouldn't be any more problems.'

'It appears you were incorrect.' Seb patted the man's arm to remind him of the situation. 'What was Thornton's response?'

'He wants me to continue monitoring the tracking device

just in case and to report to him if you come anywhere near Leicester.'

'Have you been instructed to warn or track anyone else?' Seb wanted to ensure that Daryl was being left alone.

'No. Only you two. Now, if we're done—'

'We're not,' Birdie snapped. 'What about Helen Brackstone? Did you pay her a visit all those years ago? Maybe you were meant to give her a warning as well, but things got out of hand?'

'How many times do I have to tell you? I don't know the woman and had nothing to do with her death. All I can tell you is that Thornton wants you to back off from looking into it. It's not my job to ask questions. You can forget saying I killed her because you're wrong. Who is she, anyway?'

'She was trying to prove that Roger North bribed the council to get planning permission to pull down the Riddle Park estate and put up a new development back in the late eighties. You sound local; you must have heard of the place,' Birdie said.

Pike let out a derisive chuckle. 'I remember Riddle Park. The place was a bloody cesspit. I'm surprised anyone wanted to stop it being demolished. And now I know why I've never heard of this Brackstone woman – I was banged up at Her Majesty's pleasure for over five years from the mid-eighties. But even if I was out, doing hits wasn't my style.'

'Whose style was it?' Birdie demanded. 'We want to know who Thornton or North might have hired.'

Pike snorted. 'What? You think we went out together for picnics? How the hell should I know who else they used? That's it. I'm going.' He pressed his hands down on the table, implying he was ready to leave.

Seb glanced at Birdie, who was studying the man. But she finally looked away and gave Seb a sharp nod of agreement. They'd got as much out of him as they were going to.

'Don't forget we still have the tracker with your prints on,'

Birdie reminded Pike as she got to her feet and brushed her jacket as if trying to get rid of something unpleasant. 'I also have the time and date you ran me off the road. A call to your parole officer could end up with you back inside.'

'All right, all right. No need to get nasty. I was only doing a job,' Pike said.

'A job that has come to an end,' Seb said as he stood up and loomed over Pike, choosing to use his height to intimidate the man. 'You're not to mention our chat to Thornton or North.'

Pike made a choking noise as he let out a shudder. 'No fear of that. I don't have a death wish.'

'Death wish?' Birdie spun back around. 'Are you suggesting that Thornton or North might kill you if they discovered you've talked?'

'I didn't say that.' Pike's face paled, and he shoved his phone in his pocket. 'I'm going, and I hope to hell that I never bump into you two again.'

'In which case, don't give us a reason to make another visit,' Seb said, stepping away from the table and allowing Pike to walk past.

The man tugged a flat cap onto his head and marched out of the café, not bothering to look around.

After a few seconds, Seb and Birdie followed. They headed back the way they'd walked earlier until reaching the car.

'What do you think? Was he telling the truth?' Birdie's jaw flickered and she rubbed the back of her neck.

'I suspect that he downplayed the jobs he did for Thornton. But, as far as Helen goes, he didn't seem to be lying. Of course, he wouldn't be the first criminal to orchestrate a murder from prison, but he struck me as more of a henchman than a master criminal.'

'I totally agree. For a start, why on earth would he use his own car to run me off the road? And I know we haven't checked the tracking device for fingerprints, but it was obvious from his reaction that he didn't bother to wipe it clean before fitting it to my car. Do you want to keep Pike under surveillance to see if he runs back to Thornton?'

'I don't think he will. He was too fearful,' Seb said, shaking his head.

'Of Thornton or North?' Birdie asked, drumming her fingers on her thighs.

'Maybe both.'

'It would explain why he agreed to do the job in the first place. After all, it was a risky move, considering he's on parole. Shall we pay Thornton a visit?' Birdie suggested.

'Not until we know more about him,' Seb said, starting the engine and pulling out into the traffic.

'Yeah, I suppose you're right. It's better to know what we're walking into. We can find out exactly how dirty he is, and who his illustrious clients are... You do know that, if Pike's to be believed, we're still left with the question of who drove to Market Harborough and forced the cyanide into Helen.'

TWENTY-TWO

Monday, 28 July

Birdie tapped her fingers against the office desk as she stared at another photo of William Thornton. This one had been taken at a business awards dinner ten years ago, and next to him, according to the caption underneath, was a former footballer and a cabinet minister, neither of whom Birdie recognised.

On their return from Leicester, they'd retrieved her car, removed the tracking device, and bagged it up in case it was needed as evidence. Now they were back in the office, and had been digging into the dodgy solicitor. Seb had been looking into the man's educational background and discovered that he'd been a student at Cambridge at the same time as one of his father's close friends and had stepped outside to call the man.

Birdie was concentrating on Thornton's public image and it was beginning to feel like reading a copy of *OK!* magazine. Thornton was all over the place.

She hadn't yet come across any images of Thornton and North together, but she'd made a spreadsheet to track the events they'd both attended. It was already in double digits. Was it a coincidence that they hadn't been photographed together?

Birdie added the business awards to the list and was about to close the tab when Elsa nudged open the office door with the tip of her nose and trotted in, closely followed by Seb, who was pocketing his phone.

'I found another photograph of Thornton socialising at some awards thing. I'm surprised he ever gets any work done,' she muttered. 'Did you get any dirt on him?'

'Nothing specific. Other than beneath the smooth smile, Thornton was ruthless, even as an undergraduate. I imagine the reason he attends so many events is to network for clients and, more importantly, elicit information that he might be able to use.'

'That makes sense. People can be very loose lipped after a drink or two.'

Seb joined her at the desk and studied the image on her screen. 'Those two gentlemen on either side of Thornton were involved in a scandal several years ago, which mysteriously evaporated.'

'Hmm... Interesting. I bet Thornton was the one to make it disappear. Which gives me an idea.' Birdie clicked on the name of the footballer and brought up a new window. 'I'll see if I can identify some of Thornton's previous clients. There might be other suspicious deaths we can link him to.'

'While you do that, I'm going to investigate what else was on TEC's agenda at the time in case there is another connection.'

The rest of the afternoon passed quickly, and Birdie was adding yet another past client to the list of people Thornton had represented over the years when her phone pinged with a text message. Her skin prickled. Ever since Pike had sent the threatening message, she'd been on high alert. Half expecting to receive another one.

But it was from her mum.

> I swear I'm going to run away from home if those boys don't stop leaving their dirty dishes all over the place.

Birdie replied with several crying emojis and then stood up.

It was almost seven and her shoulders and back were stiff from sitting for so long. She walked over to the French doors and stepped out onto the patio. The sun was starting to drop, but the sky was still bright as insects lazily darted around the foxgloves and lupins.

Ever since Seb had found the tracker on her car, Birdie had felt like a ticking clock had been hanging over their heads. Even if Pike kept his word and didn't tell Thornton about their conversation, the stakes had risen. If North had contacted Thornton, telling him to pass on a message to stop the investigation, it meant there might be another attempt.

Birdie was about to go back inside when Keira's car turned into the long driveway and came to a halt. At the sound of crunching tyres, Elsa ambled out and patiently waited for Keira to jog across the lawn to join them.

'Are you two still working? You do realise that it's almost seven.' Her cheeks were bright, and her long hair ruffled, as if she'd been outside in the wind. 'Does that mean you've found something?'

'A very dodgy solicitor, who could be the link we've been looking for,' Birdie said as her stomach rumbled. 'We could use a hand if you're free. I was about to suggest to your dad that we order in some food.'

'Sorry. I'm meeting some friends in an hour and desperately need a shower.' Keira shrugged and busied herself patting Elsa as Seb joined them. 'But I can do tomorrow, if that's okay?'

'Of course,' Birdie said with a smile, not wanting to make

the girl feel guilty for going out and enjoying herself. That thought suddenly made Birdie feel very old.

'You're the best.' Keira flashed her a smile. 'At least let me order you both some food. What do you fancy, Dad? Indian, Thai or... pizza?'

'Anything is fine by me,' Seb said, giving his daughter an affectionate look that made his eyes crinkle.

'I need your credit card though.'

'And here's me thinking you were going to treat us,' Seb said with a smile, as he took the card from his wallet and handed to her. 'Where are you going tonight?'

'Just to the pub,' Keira said dismissively, turning to Birdie. 'How about you? Any preferences?'

'Four seasons pizza, please. Make it extra-large and your dad and I will share.' Keira disappeared inside the house, with Elsa trailing behind. Birdie studied Seb as he checked his watch. 'You don't mind that she's busy tonight?'

Seb shook his head. 'This is our business not hers, and after the last few years, I'm pleased she's enjoying herself. How are you getting on?'

'Slowly. It would be much easier to break into Thornton's office and look at his client files. We could hire Pike to do it for us?' Seb quirked an eyebrow, and she patted his arm. 'Relax. I'm joking. How about you?'

'There are a couple of things I'm following up,' Seb said as they went inside and returned to their desks.

They briefly broke off to eat before returning to their work and it was well after nine when Seb beckoned her over to the reading corner. He was surrounded by the files Daryl had collected for them, and on the coffee table was a neatly stacked collection of folders.

'There were three other cases that TEC were investigating before Helen's death.' Seb handed her the stack. 'One was a manufacturing company accused of using underage workers.

Another a printing business that wanted to get a nearby community centre shut down, and the last one involved union workers at a construction firm, who were threatened for going on strike.'

Birdie opened the first one and scanned through it until she came to the name of the solicitor on record. Thornton. She shut the file and looked over to Seb.

'Let me guess, Thornton was involved in all three.'

'Correct. I've begun checking the three businesses, but can't find anything suspicious. How are you getting on?'

'I have eight individuals and businesses – not including the three you've found – involving Thornton. It's like he's a magnet for dodginess.' Birdie passed over her notebook where she'd jotted down the names.

Seb pursed his lips as he scanned it. A shadow crossed his face, and he looked up. 'There's a name I haven't seen in a while. Wilder Property Developers.'

'How do you know them?' Birdie's pulse hammered. The fact Seb recognised them could save hours of extra research.

'From my time at the Met. They were investigated as part of a fraud operation, but before we could get a conviction, I was seconded—'

He broke off and Birdie nodded in understanding.

Seb had been on the force for fourteen years and had been a detective inspector when he'd been shoulder-tapped to be part of a team investigating a gambling syndicate based in Singapore that was involved in a complex match-fixing network across numerous sports. The team had been close to nailing them when it was discovered one of the detective sergeants in the special squad had been leaking information.

It had blown the entire case, and the squad was disbanded. Seb resigned not long after, and while he wasn't involved in the corruption, she knew it still pained him.

'I didn't find any mention of fraud. Does that mean they were never convicted?'

He shook his head and handed back her notepad. 'Not as far as I'm aware. But it's most likely because the managing director, Leonard Peterson, died six months later. The business went into liquidation and the assets sold.'

'So, Peterson and Thornton were connected through business. Was Peterson from Leicester?'

'He had an apartment in London and a family home on the outskirts of Newtown Linford, which could explain why he used Thornton as his solicitor instead of someone from the capital.'

'This is great,' Birdie said, returning to her desk and beginning a new search. 'Right, so Peterson set up Wilder Property in 1982, which means he was around at the same time as Roger North. They were in the same area of business, both operated out of Leicester, and shared the same dodgy solicitor. Does that mean he was involved in the Camberton Towers development, do you think?'

'I didn't come across it,' Seb immediately answered, joining her at the computer. 'Do a search on Colin Howes. Peterson referred to him as his right-hand man, but the relationship appeared deeper than that.'

'Would he have committed murder for his boss, do you think?' Birdie asked, the hairs on her arms prickling.

Some people scoffed at the idea of detectives relying on their gut feelings, but she'd always found that when her heart pounded and adrenaline surged, it meant something.

'While I can't answer that question, Howes was certainly an imposing man and charges were laid against him for intimidation. They were later dropped. He lived in London during our investigation, but he was originally from Leicester.'

'Making it entirely possible that Thornton and North knew him.'

She tapped Colin Howes's name into the search bar and had to go through several pages before finding an image of him. He was mentioned in an article from twenty years ago after being involved in a car accident. Back then he'd been in his fifties with a long face and grim mouth. His eyes were narrowed, and she got the impression he didn't rely on his charm or conversation to get his own way.

'Here's our guy.'

Seb leant over to study to the screen. 'If this was taken twenty years ago, he must be in his seventies now.'

Birdie continued to scroll. There were several photos of Howes with Peterson over the years, and one taken at his former boss's funeral.

She increased the size of the photograph to see who else was in the crowd of mourners, but if Thornton or North were there, they were out of the frame.

'Hang on, let's see what happens if I search for Howes and North together.' She returned to the screen and added *Roger North* and *Fullerton Construction*, but nothing came up. She then tried Howes with Thornton.

This time, the results were better, and several images immediately appeared. Birdie clicked on the first one. It was from a race meeting, and while they weren't standing next to each other, they appeared to be with the same party.

'Excellent,' Seb said, returning to his own desk. 'It appears that Thornton knows Howes. The question remains, though, did he use Howes to do jobs in the same way he used Pike in later years?'

Birdie swivelled her chair around to face him. 'If he did, Howes might have been hired to kill Helen to stop her speaking out about Camberton Towers. I know this is all conjecture but just think if I'm right, it would mean we'd found the killer.'

'Can you find an address for Howes?'

Birdie got to work, using several programs before getting a result from the electoral roll.

'He was living in Oadby, Leicester, with his daughter and family at least until last year according to this record, so there's a good chance he's still there.'

'Excellent. North already knows we're looking into the case, but if we're lucky, he and Thornton will believe that Pike managed to scare us off. We don't want to give them a reason to think otherwise, so—'

'An early-morning surprise visit, it is,' Birdie said, interrupting and finishing Seb's sentence. 'In the meantime, I'd better get some sleep. I have the feeling that tomorrow will be an even longer day.'

TWENTY-THREE

Tuesday, 29 July

The following morning Seb and Birdie pulled up outside a large, detached house in Oadby that was set back on an upmarket street with leafy trees overhanging the wide driveway.

After Birdie had gone home the previous evening, Seb researched into Colin Howes's daughter. Alison Howes had studied medicine at Oxford and was now working as a GP.

'If Howes's daughter is here, it could be tricky,' Birdie said, echoing Seb's own thoughts.

'Yes, I realise that. We have no idea the reception we'll receive especially if she believes we're accusing her father of murder. If she's at home, that is.'

'If she is, how do you want to play it?' Birdie asked, tapping her foot on the step leading to the front door.

'We'll tell her the truth.' Seb pressed the bell and musical chimes sounded out.

Several moments later, the door cracked open. Seb recognised Alison Howes from the surgery's website where she worked. She was fifty-three, but looked younger, with blonde hair hanging down her back and a clear complexion. Her eyes were light blue but darkened as she studied them both through a chain.

'Yes?' she asked, not making any attempt to open the door further.

'My name is Sebastian Clifford, and this is my partner, Birdie. We're private investigators and would like to speak with your father, Colin, about his relationship with William Thornton.'

Alison paled, though it was unclear if it was because of her father or because they'd mentioned Thornton's name. An uneasy silence hung between them before the woman finally spoke.

'I take it you don't know.'

'Know what?' Birdie blinked.

'My father died last month. We kept it private for personal reasons. I'm still sorting through everything.'

'We're both very sorry for your loss,' Seb immediately said.

Despite their research the previous evening, they hadn't come across a death notice. It wasn't illegal to keep it out of the local papers, and it was too early for it to show up on public records even if the death had been registered. But the fact it was kept private did suggest Alison was aware of her father's past.

'Was his passing sudden?' Birdie shifted from foot to foot as the morning sun beat down on their backs.

'No, it was quite the opposite, I'm afraid. He had dementia and over the last few years had become increasingly frail. He recently broke his hip and never fully recovered.'

'That must have been painful for you and your family,' Seb said. 'We're sorry for turning up on your doorstep like this.'

'It's funny that you never know how you'll react to the death of a parent until you face it,' Alison admitted, as her hands gripped and ungripped the door with nervous energy.

'I've heard that,' Birdie said, keeping calm, with no hint of frustration that their primary lead was no longer alive. 'I know this is a difficult time, but could we ask you a few questions?'

'You said this is about William Thornton,' Alison said.

Seb nodded in agreement.

Alison took a moment to consider the request, but after a short while, she silently stepped back from the door and released the security chain. 'Come in.'

'Thank you,' Seb said.

They followed her down a wide hallway through to an open-plan kitchen at the back of the house. Light streamed in and there was a pile of folders on the long oak dining table that overlooked the rear garden.

She headed to the kettle and filled it with water, before turning back to them. Her hands were still fluttering around the handle, as if she wasn't sure what to do with them. 'I was about to make a coffee; would you like one?'

'Yes, please,' Birdie said, and Seb nodded in agreement. They made small talk until Alison joined them at the long table with the drinks. Her shoulders were looser, and she appeared more relaxed.

'I do know William Thornton. He was one of many people who used to turn up on the doorstep wanting to speak to my father, when I lived at home.'

'Please could you elaborate?' Seb asked.

'I assume that's your way of asking whether I knew the work my father did. Yes, I did. It would be hard not to, considering the numerous phone calls he received at all times of day and night.' Alison let out a bitter laugh.

'Could you tell us about your father's relationship with Thornton?' Seb asked, and Alison chewed her lip.

'I'm not sure if you've met William Thornton, but he's ruthless. If my father was still alive, we wouldn't be having this conversation.'

'Did Thornton threaten you?'

Alison shook her head. 'Not directly, but it's always been implied.'

'In what way?' Birdie asked.

'If he ever visited Dad when I was young he'd always be especially nice to me. But even then I sensed it was all a front. His smiles never quite reached his eyes, and his voice had a certain edge to it, even when he was being nice. It's hard to explain, but as a child I was always wary of him. I am still, to be honest.' Alison poured some milk into her coffee and stirred it. 'If I do talk to you, you must promise it won't go any further. He's a dangerous man.'

'You have our word that this conversation won't be repeated,' Birdie promised.

Seb put away his phone and Birdie did the same. It seemed to make a difference.

Alison swallowed and then looked directly at them both. 'My father was a fixer. He mainly worked for a man named Leonard Peterson. But from time to time, he'd receive calls from William Thornton to do jobs that—' She broke off as a flash of pain crossed her eyes. 'Well... he never went into detail, but they paid him well. My mother always said it was best not to ask questions and we should be grateful to have such a good life. After all, we had a lovely house, and I went to boarding school and from there to Oxford. I benefited directly from what he did.' She bowed her head as she spoke.

'It didn't sit well with you, though, did it?' Seb asked.

'It's taken a long time to make my peace with what my father did. Despite everything, he loved me and was incredibly proud when I got into Oxford. He was integral in making me the person I am today, which is one of the many reasons why I cared for him at home. Yet he also destroyed other people's lives. It was a challenging dichotomy.'

'Is your mother still alive?' Seb asked.

'No, she died ten years ago, and that's when my father's health started to deteriorate. Despite what he did, they loved each other. I have no siblings so sorting everything out was left to me.'

'When did you last speak to Thornton?' Seb asked.

The colour that had returned to her face drained away again. 'He phoned last week. I thought he'd heard about Dad dying and wanted to pay his respects, but it wasn't that. He was shocked when I told him.'

'What did he say?' Birdie asked.

'He said all the right things, of course, but I got the feeling he was relieved. I assumed it was because he knew about my father's failing health and quality of life. He visited occasionally, most recently after Dad broke his hip.'

'Did Thornton say anything else?' Birdie asked.

'He wanted to know if anyone had been asking after him, and I told him no, which was the truth... then. After that, he said if I needed any help with Dad's estate, he'd be happy to assist.'

'Is there any chance your father kept details regarding his work? Diaries, or even a calendar, which would help us form a timeline of events?' Seb asked hopefully.

'Yes, he had several journals. They were tatty old things, but that's because he always kept them close by. He called them his "insurance policy".'

'Wasn't that risky?' Birdie asked, with a frown.

Seb nodded. It was.

'He was prepared to take the risk. For the family.'

'Do you still have them, and could we please look? It would be a huge help,' Birdie said.

'I'm afraid I don't. A few months ago, when William Thornton visited my father, they had a private conversation and Dad gave them to him.'

'All of them?' Birdie grimaced and clamped down on her lip, as if resisting the urge to swear.

Seb didn't blame her. Without the journals they'd have no hope of discovering the involvement of Thornton and North in Helen's death. Neither of them spoke, and as the silence dragged out, Alison narrowed her eyes as she studied their reactions.

'What's this about? What case are you working on?'

Seb glanced at Birdie. It was time to explain.

'We're investigating a murder from thirty-six years ago in Market Harborough. Helen Brackstone was found poisoned in her kitchen and her husband was convicted of the crime.'

Alison's brows pressed together and her eyes were thoughtful. 'I'm sorry, I don't recognise the name.'

'You didn't hear your parents mention the name at all?' Birdie asked.

'Not that I recall, but my mother didn't ask questions, as I've already mentioned.' Alison sucked in a breath, as if bracing herself for bad news. 'Are you suggesting my father was involved in this woman's death?'

'That's what we're here to find out,' Seb explained. He told her about Daryl and her wish to clear her father's name. 'I'm sorry if this is painful.'

'To be honest, it's almost a relief. All these years, it's felt like I've been waiting for the other shoe to drop. While I'm finally at peace with what my father did, it's better I know the truth. Especially if an innocent man was wrongly convicted.' She shifted in her chair, her fingers weaving together, unable to hide her discomfort.

'We appreciate your cooperation. It's a pity we're too late to see the journals. If Thornton took them away, it suggests there was compromising information in them. I imagine he would have destroyed them by now,' Seb said.

'You're probably right,' Alison agreed, her gaze frank, 'Which is why I made copies of them.'

'You *what?*' Birdie's entire face lit up.

'I'm not proud of it. Whatever my father did, I always respected his privacy, but as the dementia took hold, he started to let things slip. I was never sure if they were real events, or figments of his imagination.'

'He admitted everything to you?' Birdie asked, her eyes wide.

'Not exactly, but he appeared tormented. It made me think of Dickens's Scrooge, and that he was being visited by the ghosts of his past.'

'That must have been difficult for you to witness.'

'It was. Last year, when he was in hospital he began to fret because the journals were hidden in his wardrobe. He couldn't settle and kept dreaming someone would break in and steal them. That if the truth got out it would harm my family and—' She broke off and turned away. 'Until then, I'd forgotten of their existence, but on his second day in the ward, he made me promise to put them in the safe, so no one could get them.'

'Did you read them?' Birdie asked.

'No.' Alison shut her eyes and a flash of pain crossed her face. 'It seems I'm more of my mother's daughter than I'd like to admit. I found the journals on the wardrobe shelf, covered by an old moth-eaten jumper. I couldn't even bring myself to touch them without wearing gloves. I put them in the wall safe and told my father where they were.'

'What made you decide to copy them?'

'That night I ended up being the one who couldn't sleep. My father had forty years of knowing what was in them and I couldn't even last one night. I decided to copy them so that even if the journals were taken, or went missing, I'd still have the insurance he'd wanted. I couldn't let anything happen to my family.'

'Did you read them?' Birdie asked.

'I started to... but – and you'll think I'm crazy – I couldn't get beyond the first couple of pages. I couldn't face seeing my dad in a different light. It was different vaguely knowing what he did, from actually reading about it in his own writing... I couldn't bear it. Does that make me a coward?'

'Your reaction is understandable,' Seb assured her. 'You're the opposite of a coward and that's why you copied the dairies. It's why you agreed to talk to us. I won't pretend to understand what you're going through, but Birdie and I have worked enough cases to know that people show their true characters when things become difficult.'

'Seb's right. It's clear you've spent a lot of time trying to come to terms with your father and his job. By helping us now, we might be able to give that same peace of mind to someone else,' Birdie added.

The room fell silent as they gave Alison time to process their words. Finally, she stood and walked over to a section of the wall and pressed one of the panels. The moulded segment swung back to reveal a safe. She tapped in a code and silently opened it. She returned several moments later with two large envelopes.

'These are all the pages. I hope you'll find something that can give your client answers, about what happened to her family. It will make whatever you find out about my father easier to bear.'

Seb took the thick envelopes from her. Colin Howes clearly had many secrets.

'Thank you.' Birdie handed Alison a business card. 'We'll return these to you soon. If you have any questions, please call. Or if you hear from William Thornton. We believe that he thinks we're no longer pursuing the case, so you should be safe.'

Alison walked them to the front door. 'Please keep me posted on what you discover.'

'Of course,' Birdie assured her.

They returned to the car, and Seb discreetly scanned the street for any signs they were being watched. He then checked the car for a tracking device, which also proved negative, before finally climbing in.

'Now, let's return to the office and go through the journal pages.'

TWENTY-FOUR

Tuesday, 29 July

Birdie shifted awkwardly in the wrought-iron patio chair later that afternoon. It dug into her spine as she tried to get comfortable. She suspected that part of her discomfort was from reading Colin Howes's journals. The trouble was, Howes had written pages of details for each event but he hadn't bothered to date any of them, which meant they couldn't narrow the search down to the days surrounding Helen's death.

They'd been at it for over two hours and Seb was still in the office. She'd come outside, hoping the warm summer air would be a counter to reading about Howes's dark deeds. It wasn't working, and she rolled her shoulders. The two envelopes Alison Howes had given them contained almost four hundred pages of notes, most of them relating to when Howes worked for Leonard Peterson in London, but interspersed were visits back to Leicester where he'd regularly met up with Thornton and North.

Sighing, Birdie picked up the next page and skimmed

through it, by now familiar with Howes's casual way of writing about the many jobs he had done for his various employers.

Visited a couple of likely lads in Manchester who thought they could get away without paying their tab. Worked them over a little too hard. But the boss always says it's better to do too much rather than not enough. They won't try crossing us again.

It should have been called 'Journal of a Hitman'. Birdie dreaded to think what he might have been like if social media had been around at the time. Would he have made a podcast about the best way to kneecap someone using a baseball bat?

She picked up the next page as Seb joined her on the patio. His jaw was set in a grim line. It appeared he was finding it as difficult as she was.

'Got anything? Or have you had enough?' she asked as he passed over two of the pages in his hand.

'Both. I've found what we were looking for, but it doesn't make for easy reading.'

Birdie swallowed and took the sheets of paper. Finding the truth often meant digging into the worst parts of people. But without it, nothing would change.

She ran a hand along the back of her neck and studied the page.

New job from Thornton. North has been having problems with that fancy development of his. Not sure why anyone would care about saving Riddle Park. The place was a bloody dump. Good riddance to Riddle. Some mob called TEC are sticking their noses in and stirring up trouble. North could lose millions if they don't back off. Tomorrow, Thornton and I are going for a day trip to Market Harborough. It must be serious for Thornton to come with me. Usually I'm left to deal with things alone. He wants to scare the crap out of some silly housewife who has too much time on her hands.

A combination of anger and sadness raced through Birdie. It was what they'd been looking for, but now that they'd found it...

'Are you okay?' Seb checked. 'I can give you the shortened version if you don't want to read the rest.'

'I'm fine... but how can he write so calmly about what he does? All for the sake of money.'

'For some people, that's all there is. It's how they measure their value in the world, and how they define success.'

'Yeah, well, it will be my great delight to prove them wrong,' Birdie muttered, turning to the second page.

What a cock up. Went to pay Helen Brackstone a visit with Thornton. I was surprised she even let us in the house. It was a nice place and not what I was expecting. But instead of slamming the door in our face, she eyed Thornton up and said she knew exactly who he was. She was even smiling. I reckon she wanted the chance to ask him questions. I could've told her that wouldn't work. But she wasn't the one paying me... Thornton and North were, so in we went and got comfortable.

The plan was to scare her off, but she wouldn't play ball, so Thornton told me to get heavy. I refused. I don't do over women or kids. There were photos on the wall of a girl. Probably about the same age as my Alison. Well... I couldn't do it.

Instead, I told her that if she loved her family, she should listen to Thornton. But the stupid cow wouldn't. She kept saying over and over that it was up to her to stop men like North from getting away with things. She had proof that he'd bribed the planning committee to get the development passed.

I told her she was delusional. Of course, they could get away with it because they had money, and she didn't. I said that she was a bug under their feet, and if she didn't back off, she'd be squashed. If only she'd listened.

Thornton made me tie her up in a chair. I thought he was going to smack her around a bit. But then he pulled something out of his coat pocket and shoved it into her mouth. Turned out it was a bloody cyanide capsule. It's not what I'd do. Poison's a woman's game. For someone who doesn't want to get their hands dirty. It was all over before I knew it.

I wanted to take the body and dump it, but Thornton said no because he was going to frame the husband. I untied her and made it look like she'd been drinking a coffee. I checked the shed and found some weedkiller with enough cyanide in it, so we didn't even need to plant it. We let ourselves out like we'd never been there, and I went home and drank myself stupid.

Birdie pushed the page to one side and closed her eyes, letting the warmth of the sun try to take away the chill that had reached her bones. Neither of them spoke for a long while.

Finally, she opened her eyes and glanced over at Seb. He was holding several more sheets of paper.

'I take it there are more entries.'

'Yes. Maurice Bryant's name comes up – Howes paid him several visits. There was nothing to connect him to Bryant's death, but it seems likely he was behind that as well.'

'More lives ruined.' Birdie clenched her fists, more determined to get justice, no matter how late it was. 'Anything else?'

'Yes. Mainly regarding fitting up Wes,' Seb told her. 'Thornton told Howes he had a detective on the take in Market Harborough, and that he would ensure that Wes was the only suspect.'

'Did Howes give the detective's name?'

'He said that Thornton wasn't one to give much away, but he once let it slip that the detective's initials were JD.'

'Jeff Dunbar. Twiggy was convinced he was on the take. We saw for ourselves how he changed tactics in his notebook. That slimy little—' She broke off and tapped the table. There was no point getting annoyed at the crooked officer. 'Shall we take this straight to Twig?'

'No. We'll visit Dunbar ourselves to see if we can get him to admit it. Considering what we now know, he was surprisingly willing to cooperate with us last time.'

'Maybe he wants to gloat that he'd got away with it. That or he has a guilty conscience and wants to get caught?' Birdie raised an eyebrow. 'If it's the latter it would certainly explain why he answered our questions and handed over his notebooks.'

'I think he's got a guilty subconscious,' Seb said as he got to his feet. 'We have a better chance of discovering the truth with a private visit. Once the police are involved, he might clam up.'

'Good point. We're going to need as much proof as possible. Journal entries will only get us so far, especially as they're not dated.'

'I agree, but the evidence is certainly mounting. We have the tracker on your car and Pike's ankle monitor records should confirm he was the one to drive you off the road. We also know that Thornton called Alison Howes, hoping to have a chat with Colin, which suggests he was worried we might contact his *fixer*.'

'And all of this happened after we contacted North,' Birdie added, picking up on his line of thought. 'I reckon North got off the phone to us and immediately called his old friend Thornton, warning him that someone was digging into the past and that it needed sorting out. Just like they did with Helen and Maurice Bryant.'

'We have our phone records to prove when we called

North, but if we could get access to North's outgoing calls, it would tie him back to everything. Or if there are other calls as well.' The grim lines around Seb's mouth were replaced by the hint of a smile.

He didn't show his emotions often, but it seemed he was as determined as she was to make those men pay.

'Which is why you're smirking. Because when you spoke to Rob the other day, he told you that someone was still keeping tabs on North.'

'I wouldn't call it *smirking*,' Seb protested as he pulled out his phone. 'But yes. I'm going to enquire if there have been any recent calls between the two men. We know how far the pair of them went the last time to cover their tracks, and I don't trust them not to do the same again.'

Birdie pushed back her chair and stood. 'While you call Rob, I'll map out a timeline so we can expose exactly where Dunbar's story falls apart. Let's see him talk his way out of that.'

TWENTY-FIVE

Wednesday, 30 July

For the second time in two days, Seb parked outside the well-maintained bungalow in Wilby. They'd driven there yesterday afternoon, not wanting to give Dunbar any advance warning, but the place had been empty, and after waiting an hour for him to appear, they'd called it a day and returned to East Farndon. They'd spent the rest of the evening going through the evidence to ensure nothing was missed.

Seb hadn't yet heard back from Rob regarding accessing North's phone records to discover if any calls were made to Thornton. His friend had given him a gentle reminder that if they had proof North was behind a murder, the case must be handed over to the police. Seb had immediately agreed. He had no interest in becoming a rogue detective, but equally, he wasn't prepared to leave any loose ends in case it resulted in the murderer escaping conviction.

'Fingers crossed we're second-time lucky,' Birdie said, climbing out of the car and slinging her bag over one shoulder.

Her mouth was set in a determined line, and her eyes were clear and focused.

Seb walked behind as she marched down the short path and to the front door. This time, the sound of the radio could be heard from behind the door, and Dunbar appeared not long after she'd knocked. There was an apron wrapped around his waist, and his green eyes flickered with surprise.

'I didn't expect to see you two again.'

'Really? Why's that?' Birdie asked, the bright smile on her face at odds with her pointed glare.

Dunbar didn't appear perturbed as he removed his apron, dropped it down on the small table in the hall, and ushered them inside and through to his small lounge.

'You're working a cold case and it stands to reason that you'll realise it's a waste of time. It was an open-and-shut case and the jury found Wes Brackstone guilty in record time. That doesn't happen for nothing. What's this about?' Dunbar sat down in his armchair, this time not offering them a drink.

'We have a few more questions. I take it you don't mind me recording your responses?' Birdie held up her phone.

'Do what you want. I've got nothing to hide.'

'Good to know.' Birdie set her phone to record and placed it on the coffee table.

Dunbar watched calmly. If he was rattled by their visit, he didn't show it. His eyes were more curious than nervous. Unless he was acting. It wouldn't surprise Seb, considering the number of years he'd had to get his story straight.

'Right. We're recording now.' Birdie returned to sitting on the sofa and stared directly at Dunbar.

'We've discovered who killed Helen Brackstone... and it wasn't her husband, Wes,' Seb informed him.

Dunbar was silent as he rubbed his chin, his gaze meeting theirs. 'I see. Why do you think that?'

'We don't *think* it, we *know* it,' Birdie snapped, her patience clearly coming to an end.

'My mistake,' Dunbar quickly backtracked. 'Who's this other killer, then?'

'We'll get to that.' Seb fixed him with a cool smile. He wasn't interested in letting the ex-detective lead the conversation. 'First, we want to discuss why Wes was the only person you suspected.'

'I've already told you. It was where the evidence pointed. Look, I was a rookie back then, but the guv was a good detective. He knew what he was doing and I had no reason to believe otherwise, he—'

'Do you think he was on the take?' Birdie interrupted so quickly that Dunbar's eye twitched several times before his genial mask reappeared.

Seb silently praised his partner for her ability to throw the man off-kilter.

'What? You think DI Best took backhanders?'

'Do *you*?' Seb countered.

Dunbar's eye twitched again and Birdie let out a low breath. She'd noted it as well. Finally, the man's true character was surfacing.

'I'm not saying Best was on the take... but I suppose it's possible. He had a young family and one of the kids was in a wheelchair. There were hospital bills. Things the health service wouldn't pay for,' Dunbar said, fixing them with a frank stare, as if he was only talking to them because they were all friends.

'Interesting. Did you ever witness Best taking a bribe?' Birdie pushed.

Dunbar's brow puckered as if it was costing him something to answer the question. Seb wasn't fooled; it was clearly an act for their benefit.

'No, but I wasn't looking for it, was I? It was different back then. The country was a mess, wages were rubbish, and there was no CCTV. No civilians with camera phones trying to record your every move. If extra money was offered, I can see how *some* people might have been tempted.'

'But not you, of course,' Birdie said, her tone sarcastic.

Dunbar stiffened, and his mouth opened. 'I don't like what you're suggesting.'

'Which is what?' Birdie said, feigning innocence, her hand fluttering by her chest.

'If I was bent, I'd hardly invite you into my home. Twice. Or let you go through my notebooks. Only an idiot would do that.' Dunbar folded his arms and stared smugly at Birdie.

'Yet, you haven't asked us who gave the backhander to ensure Wes Brackstone was convicted,' Seb pointed out.

'That is strange,' Birdie agreed. 'Surely, if you were innocent, you'd want to know *who* was behind it.'

Dunbar's fingers tightened around the curved arms of the chair. They'd rattled him.

'Okay, so tell me. Who wanted us to convict the wrong man?' Dunbar said.

'William Thornton,' Birdie said, her voice flat.

'Never heard of him,' Dunbar snapped, a little too quickly.

'Nice try,' Birdie said, leaning forward. 'Thornton's fixer, Colin Howes, kept a detailed journal of all his *jobs* and your name appears several times. Does that jog your memory?'

'Howes? Are you serious? That guy worked for anyone who paid. As for a journal – do me a favour, he was hardly the literary type.'

'Guess it takes all sorts,' Birdie retorted.

Dunbar suddenly lunged to one side, fumbling for his mobile phone on the table, but all he managed to do was send it flying onto the floor.

Birdie jumped to her feet and crossed the room in three fast strides, all before the ex-policeman could manoeuvre himself out of his chair.

'Do you want to call someone?' Birdie asked, picking up the phone and waving it in front of Dunbar, whose face was now a mottled shade of red. 'Don't let us stop you. In fact, you haven't even locked it, which means I can get into your address book. Who shall I look for? Thornton? While I'm at it, I'll check your recent call history, too.'

'All right, all right. You two think you're so clever, don't you?' Dunbar said, but the fight was gone out of him and he leant back in his chair.

'I suggest you tell us the truth,' Seb said.

'And stitch myself up?' Dunbar glanced at Birdie's phone, which was still recording every word.

'You did that in 1989 when you helped put an innocent man behind bars,' Birdie growled. 'We already have what we need. The question is how far your involvement went and whether we can charge you as an accessory to the murder of Helen Brackstone. Then let's see how much fun your retirement is.'

'Accessory?' Dunbar exploded. 'That murder had nothing to do with me. I don't even know what happened.'

'Whether true or not, you obstructed justice, which we can prove,' Seb snapped, his patience wearing thin. 'For your own sake, I suggest you talk us through what really happened.'

A wave of dislike flashed across Dunbar's face. Had he now realised that he wasn't as clever as he thought he was?

'Okay. This is the truth. I met Thornton in the pub, a year before Helen's murder. He said he'd slip me a couple of notes if I could give him some information on an upcoming case. It was easy money and didn't harm anyone. This happened a few times, but it wasn't until the murder that he asked me to ignore evidence.'

'And you agreed,' Birdie stated, shaking her head.

'I had no choice. If I'd refused he'd have informed the boss and I'd have been out on my ear. Looking back, he was grooming me to do his bidding. I was a young fool.'

'Did Thornton explain why he wanted the evidence ignored?' Seb asked.

'He said if Wes *wasn't* convicted a lot of people would lose money... and that it would be worth my while to do what he asked.'

'Did DI Best know you were being paid off?'

'You're joking, aren't you?' Dunbar let out a snort. 'Best wasn't like that. He was a thorough bastard. Which proves it could have been Wes, anyway. No smoke without fire, and all that. All I had to do was downplay any mention of TEC, or the Camberton Towers development. It really wasn't hard and I didn't think it harmed anyone.'

Seb shook his head in disbelief at Dunbar's dismissive words. 'What about Rosemary Fry's testimony? She told us that the police went to her house and encouraged her to change her statement to make sure that no one else was murdered in their own home.'

'You have been busy, haven't you?' Dunbar sneered. 'Look... I might've leant on a couple of the witnesses, but I didn't put words into their mouths.'

'Did you continue working for Thornton after this?' Birdie asked.

Birdie had mentioned Twiggy's long-held suspicions that Dunbar was on the take, so her question was obviously for her old partner.

Dunbar shrugged. 'Sure. Though nothing like that again. Just the occasional piece of information and evidence being mislaid. It was much easier in those days before everyone wanted to go paperless.'

'Everything has a ripple effect,' Seb retorted, remembering his own time at the Met.

'After you retired, who took over as Thornton's lackey?' Birdie asked.

'Settle down. It's not like I was selling state secrets,' Dunbar snapped, rolling his eyes.

'You didn't answer my question.'

'No one in Market Harborough, but maybe someone in Leicester. I don't know for sure. What happens now?'

'I think you know the answer to that,' Birdie said. 'Unless you have any evidence for us that links Thornton to Helen's murder. That might make the Crown Prosecution Service be inclined to look on you more favourably.'

Dunbar closed his eyes and swallowed hard, as if accepting the reality of what he'd done.

'Everything was done in person, using cash. There was no trail. I couldn't afford it, in case my role was discovered. It suited Thornton, too.'

'Did Thornton ever mention Roger North? Or did you meet him?'

Dunbar paled. 'I've never met him...'

'But clearly you know of him,' Birdie said.

'Only from the odd thing Thornton said. I wouldn't say he feared North, but his voice changed whenever his name was mentioned. You think North was involved in the murder, too?'

'It's part of our investigation,' Birdie replied.

'In that case, I've said enough. Leave.' Dunbar pointed at the door.

'We're going. I need some fresh air.' Birdie stabbed at the screen of Dunbar's phone and then tossed it back to him. 'I've deleted Thornton's number as a reminder not to call him, because if you do, it will make things worse.'

Birdie scooped up her own phone, which was still recording, and returned it to her jacket pocket.

Once they were back in the car and heading towards the

police station, she exhaled loudly. 'Do you think we have enough to convince Sarge to open the case and charge Dunbar?'

'I do.' Seb pressed his foot down on the accelerator. 'We have his confession recorded on your phone.'

'Did you notice his surprise when he finally realised he'd been busted? It's like he believed he didn't do anything wrong.'

'He's no doubt told himself the same story for so long that he believed it. Maybe it helped him sleep better at night...'

Birdie pulled out her mobile. 'I'll call Twig and let him know we're on our way.'

TWENTY-SIX

Wednesday, 30 July

When Birdie and Seb arrived at the station, they went with Twiggy to Sarge's office, though neither spoke much as she and Seb walked them through the evidence and played them the recording of the interview they'd had with Dunbar

'That little piece of—' Twiggy cut himself off as the recording finished playing, his face set in an angry scowl. 'He didn't even sound sorry that an innocent man died in jail.'

'Seb reckons that over the years, he started believing his own lies.' Birdie picked up a pencil from the desk and spun it in her fingers.

'Good work, you two. I always knew Dunbar was bent but had no evidence,' Twiggy said gruffly. 'Do you think he'll go squealing to Thornton? I know he said he wouldn't, but since I wouldn't trust him as far as I could throw him, I don't find it reassuring.'

'I suspect he'll be too worried that Thornton will send someone over to deal with him,' Seb said.

'Let's hope you're right,' Twiggy said.

'I agree with Clifford,' Sarge said, leaning forward and snatching the pencil out of Birdie's hand before she could spin it again. 'I forgot what a pain in my arse you could be.'

'What's a little pencil twirling between friends?' Birdie blew him a kiss, knowing how much it would annoy him. 'Besides, we've brought you a huge case that will bring kudos to the department and I'm sure you don't have historic murder investigations coming out of your ears.'

'No, just hairs.' Twiggy chortled before Sarge gave him a thunderous glare. Twiggy quickly pressed his lips together. 'Er, just joking. What do you want to do about Thornton? Shall I take Tiny with me and bring him in for questioning?'

Sarge shook his head. 'Not yet. We'll bring Dunbar in for questioning tomorrow and then decide our next move. As a retired officer, he should be interviewed by a more senior officer, but the higher-ups are away on a budget conference, so it's down to us. I doubt anyone from Professional Standards will be able to attend, either, because they're so busy but I'll check. We also need to interview Pike.'

At the mention of Pike's name, Twiggy's face darkened. 'Don't think I didn't make the connection, Birdie. You called me to check the plates, but failed to mention he'd run you off the road.'

'Because I was fine and didn't want you to worry.'

'I worry when you make harebrained decisions,' Twiggy retorted. 'Like being run off the road and not telling anyone.'

'I promise that next time it happens, you can drop everything and rescue me,' Birdie quipped, fixing him with an equally annoyed stare. 'Don't worry, Seb's already read me the Riot Act. Thanks for following up with Pike. It won't take much leaning to get him to talk.'

'Speaking of leaning,' Sarge broke in. 'This is now officially a police investigation and I don't want either of you going near any of the suspects or making further contact with Thornton or North.'

'They're all yours,' Seb assured him. 'Though, with your permission, we'd like to observe the interviews so we can report back to Daryl on the outcome of our investigation into her mother's murder.'

Sarge raised a bushy eyebrow. 'In other words, you want to use that memory of yours to record the entire thing.'

'I will use my discretion,' Seb assured him. 'We'll inform her that even if Thornton and Howes are sentenced and her father's conviction is posthumously overturned, it's a lengthy progress and there are no guarantees.'

Sarge was silent, and Birdie leant in closer. 'Come on, Sarge. I think we've earnt the right to see this thing through. We'll even bring our own coffee.'

'That's because the stuff here tastes like mud,' Twiggy retorted.

Sarge ignored him, but slowly nodded his head. 'Fine. I'll get our resident comedian here to let you know once Dunbar's been picked up.' He fixed Birdie with a sharp glare. 'We won't delay proceedings if you decide to turn up late.'

Birdie grinned and got to her feet. 'Relax. I'm practically a reformed woman. Isn't that right, Seb?'

'Practically,' Seb agreed, joining her by the door. He nodded at Sarge and Twiggy. 'Don't worry. We'll be here before you start. Call us if any of our case notes need clarifying.'

'Will do. Now, everyone, get out of my office so I can think in peace,' Sarge growled.

Once they'd left the office, they made their farewells to Twiggy and headed downstairs and out to the car.

Seb's mouth was set in a pensive line and Birdie frowned. 'Is everything okay?' she asked. 'Are you worried Dunbar might contact Thornton?'

'I'm not happy when things are left to chance. I'll be relieved once the pair of them are in custody. Despite our evidence, it's not a foregone conclusion that they'll be convicted.'

It was true. But they'd done as much as they could. It was time to sit back and relax.

Birdie clicked her seatbelt in place, as her phone buzzed with a text message.

> I just got asked by someone if I could help them find a book with a blue cover that might have been about an elephant. I hope your day has been a bit less weird.

Birdie read the message again and smiled to herself. Since Melinda had first asked her on the date, there had been no pressure at all. Instead, she'd let Birdie go at her own pace. Now the case was all but over, Birdie had more free time, and what better way to celebrate?

And she really did need to find out if Melinda managed to find the blue-covered book in question.

> You know you shouldn't tease a detective with an unsolved mystery. Why don't we meet up tonight at the pub? Just the two of us…

She hit send. Melinda's reply came back almost immediately.

> See you at 7. Can't wait.

'You look pleased with yourself,' Seb commented as he headed towards East Farndon.

'You should keep your eyes on the road,' Birdie retorted, not bothering to answer his question. Instead, she closed her eyes and allowed herself another smile. All in all, it was turning into a good day.

TWENTY-SEVEN

Thursday, 31 July

Dunbar had dressed for the occasion, and as Birdie stared at him through the one-way glass of the interview room the following morning, her dislike increased. The jeans and T-shirt had been replaced with a suit and tie and a bemused expression played on his lips, as if he had no idea what he was doing in there.

'What a piece of work, looking all mystified like our conversation with him yesterday never happened.' Birdie clenched a fist, pleased she didn't need to hide her distaste for the man.

'He's had all evening to consider his position.' Seb took a sip of the coffee they'd picked up before walking into Market Harborough Police Station. 'Remember, he's had years of hiding that he was in Thornton's pocket. I'm not surprised it comes easily to him.'

'Which makes me dislike him even more.' Birdie drained her own coffee as Sarge and Twiggy took their seats in the two chairs opposite Dunbar.

Twiggy pressed the recording button. 'Interview on the

thirty-first of July. Those present are Detective Sergeant Weston, Detective Constable Branch, and—' He paused and turned his head to where Dunbar was studying them with puzzled curiosity. 'Please state your name for the recording.'

'Jeffrey Simon Dunbar.' He folded his arms in front of his chest. 'Now perhaps you can tell me what the hell you were playing at, coming to my house early this morning in a marked car and dragging me from my bed?'

'It was gone nine when my officers arrived,' Sarge corrected. 'We'd like to discuss the death of Helen Brackstone. She was found dead in her home on the fifteenth of May, 1989. You were one of the detectives on the case.'

'Was I? That's a long time ago. These days I can hardly remember what I had for breakfast. Not that I had any today, thanks to your manhandling.'

'If you're hungry, we can arrange for some toast,' Twiggy assured him. 'But it might take a while. In the meantime, let's chat. Did you receive a phone call from William Thornton before you arrived at the victim's house, or while you were on the scene?'

'Sorry, I can't help you.' Dunbar shrugged, but the muscles in his cheek flickered. '1989 was a long time ago, and I was only a DC back then, not the lead detective. But you know all about that, don't you, *Detective Constable* Branch?'

Twiggy stiffened and Birdie sucked in a breath. 'Keep it together, Twig,' she muttered. 'You've never even wanted promotion.'

'Don't worry, he's got it under control,' Seb assured her.

Birdie could only see Twiggy's back, but as she watched, he visibly relaxed.

'I sure do. Yet, as a lowly DC, I've still never forgotten my first murder investigation. Let's try again, shall we?' Twiggy said.

Birdie turned to Seb, and her mouth dropped in surprise.

'Since when you do know Twiggy better than I do? Okay, I get that you're on better terms these days, but I didn't think you got on that well.'

'I've started to appreciate Twiggy's rather unique approach to policing,' Seb replied with a shrug. 'He might act like a grumpy, laid-back detective who would rather be eating lunch than working, but underneath, he knows exactly what he's doing.'

'Well... most of the time he does. Sometimes he's just irritating. But he is very fond of eating.' Birdie swallowed, an unexpected wave of sadness hitting her that Seb had been able to sum up her friend so well. Even though Twiggy's FTD meant that one day it might change.

Birdie turned her attention back to the interview.

'I repeat, when did William Thornton instruct you to make sure Wes Brackstone was implicated for his wife's murder?' Twiggy asked in an unruffled tone. 'If you need me to jog your memory further, William Thornton is the solicitor who'd been paying you for years to be an informant.'

'So, not a question, but an accusation?' Dunbar countered, but the muscle in his cheek continued to twitch.

'That's it. Keep pushing.' Birdie put down her coffee cup and folded her arms, while next to her, Seb's mouth was drawn into a tight line.

'Accusation? I think there's been some confusion which can be easily resolved,' Sarge cut in. He opened the folder on the table and pulled out a piece of paper. 'Right: "I met Thornton in the pub, a year before the Brackstone murder. He said he'd slip me a couple of notes if I could give him some information on an upcoming case. It was easy money and didn't harm anyone. This happened a few times, but it wasn't until the Brackstone murder that he asked me to ignore evidence."'

'That's a direct quote from your interview with Birdie and

Clifford yesterday,' Twiggy said. 'It was taken from a recording that you gave permission for them to make.'

'Is it? I don't remember,' Dunbar said, a self-satisfied smile spreading across his face.

'You can *not remember* all you like but we have a copy of the recording. Why did you admit to everything yesterday, knowing it would get back to us?' Twiggy asked.

'I think we both know the answer to that question.'

'Cut the crap, Dunbar,' Twiggy snapped.

'Okay, let's take this down a notch,' Sarge said, sounding much friendlier than usual. 'You want immunity from prosecution, is that correct?'

'Yes. And if my hands weren't chained together, I would clap.'

'For the record, Jeffrey Dunbar's hands are not cuffed, and he has free movement during this interview,' Sarge stated.

Sarge placed the paper in the folder and sat still. It was as if they were playing chess. The silence was almost unbearable.

Birdie clenched and unclenched her fists. Surely they had enough against Thornton with Howes's journals and their research into the planning applications not to need Dunbar's testimony? She hated that there was still a chance he could get off.

'Come on, Dunbar,' Sarge finally said. 'You know as well as I do how these things work. Answer our questions and then we can go to the Crown Prosecution Service for a decision regarding your prosecution. They won't decide without first seeing the evidence.'

'Not good enough. If you want me to talk about anything other than how worried I am about not taking my medication on time because of missing breakfast, I suggest you contact the CPS and get back to me.'

'Even if they agree, it will still depend on *what* you tell us.'

'Then I had better make sure it's worth your while.' Dunbar

leant back in his chair and rubbed his wrists, as if they had in fact been in cuffs.

'Interview suspended,' Sarge said.

Sarge and Twiggy left the room, leaving Dunbar alone. Once the door closed, Dunbar stared directly ahead. Did he know Birdie and Seb were watching? The quick tip of his head in their direction suggested that he did.

'I hate that he's playing us,' Birdie said, glaring back at him before leaving the observation area to join Twiggy and Sarge in the corridor.

'I wouldn't phrase it quite like that. I'm sure this is far from the outcome he would've preferred. Even if he gets immunity and keeps his police pension, he'll lose any standing he once might have had with people in the force,' Seb reassured her.

'Yes, but he won't be in prison,' Birdie said as they reached Sarge and Twiggy. 'Were you planning to offer him immunity?' she asked her former colleagues.

'It depended on him. We certainly weren't going to offer it up front.' Sarge's calm smile was gone, and his usual gruff frown had returned.

It helped abate Birdie's own anger, and she took a shuddering breath while next to her Twiggy patted her arm.

'If I resisted the urge to punch him,' he said, 'then so can you. Besides, there was something satisfying about seeing the bent git sitting across the table from us. He might not have shown it, but on the inside, he'd have been seething. Especially being questioned by a lowly DC.'

'You're right. His face when you didn't rise to his jibe was priceless.' Birdie let out a chuckle as Seb fell into step with Sarge on their way back to the office.

'Do you think the CPS will agree?' Seb asked.

'That's what I'm about to find out,' Sarge said. 'I've already been in touch and informed them there's compelling proof the case needs reopening. Once I have their decision, I'll interview

Dunbar again. I take it you both want to be here for round two?'

'Wouldn't miss it for the world,' Birdie assured him.

Once Sarge had left, grumbling under his breath, the three of them sat around Twiggy's desk. 'How long do you reckon it will take?' Birdie asked.

'How long's a piece of string?' Twiggy shrugged before giving her a reluctant smile. 'But I hope it's not too quick. I want Dunbar to sweat.'

'I suspect he already is. Was he serious about needing his medication?' Seb asked, his brows knitted together. In the past, Twiggy would have stiffened and said something sharp in response, but instead, he shook his head.

'Not as far as we know. He told us he only took tablets at teatime,' Twiggy answered and then lapsed into silence.

Seb turned and examined the wall, and Birdie bit back a smile. While the simmering tension between her old and new partners had lessened, it was clear they were never going to be buddies who chatted.

'So, what have you both got planned for the weekend?' Birdie said to break the silence. 'I've got a home game, which should be a cracker, and then I'm off to view a shoebox that's masquerading as a two-bedroom townhouse...'

By the time Sarge reappeared an hour later, Birdie was the first to jump out of her chair and race over to him, pleased the wait was over.

'So? What did they say? Why didn't you come in sooner and give us an update?' The words tumbled from her mouth.

'And miss watching you tear around my station like a toddler on a sugar rush?' Sarge raised one eyebrow. 'We can offer Dunbar immunity, obviously dependent on what information he gives. We'll interview him now. Come on, Twiggy. We'll stop at my office on the way to collect the case folder.'

The DC pulled on his jacket before joining Sarge, leaving Birdie and Seb to make their own way.

Back in the observation area, Birdie stared through the one-way glass at Dunbar. He was seated in the same chair and looked as if he hadn't moved. Next to him was a plate, on which sat the remains of a sandwich and a half-drunk bottle of water.

'Let the games begin,' she said with a wry smile.

Sarge and Twiggy entered the room and the interview was restarted.

'But it will be off the table unless you fully cooperate,' Sarge said after updating Dunbar on his conversation with the CPS.

'I'm a man of my word.' Dunbar held up his hands, as if trying to reassure them. 'What do you want to know?'

'When did Thornton contact you?'

Dunbar sat back in his chair, appearing relaxed. 'Thornton phoned me at the station before the murder was called in. He told me to make sure I was allocated to the case and to ensure the husband was charged. We were short-staffed back then, so I knew I'd be sent out. It wasn't a problem.'

'Did you ask him why?' Sarge asked.

'No. But even if he hadn't called, it was a no-brainer. It was already pointing to the husband. There were a few inconsistencies with the neighbours, but I sorted it out.'

'What about other leads? Did you consider Helen's involvement with TEC?' Sarge asked.

Dunbar shrugged. 'Like I said, we were short-staffed, and Best never commented when I didn't add it to the case notes. All I did was nudge the case along. Let's face it, Brackstone was low-hanging fruit and we got our conviction without too much effort.'

'Did Thornton tell you who murdered Helen?' Sarge asked.

'No. For all I knew, her husband did actually kill her and Thornton had wanted to make sure justice was served.'

'Do you expect me to believe that?' Sarge asked, his arms folded.

'I don't care one way or another.'

'For the record, you received a phone call asking for your interference in a case and you went along with the request... without asking any questions?' Sarge shook his head.

Dunbar licked his lips. 'Later that day, Thornton called and explained there was a big deal going down that could potentially fall through if we started digging into the wrong areas. He paid well... so I let it slide.'

'How were you paid?' Twiggy asked.

'Cash. Monthly. The amount varied depending on what Thornton had wanted me to do.'

'How long did these payments continue?'

'Until I retired,' Dunbar admitted.

'You must have missed the money,' Twiggy said.

'Yeah... but what could I do?'

'I don't believe him,' Birdie said, turning to Seb. 'I reckon he's still on the payroll. Thornton still needs to ensure his silence... except he's talking to us now.' She pulled out her phone and sent a text to Twiggy.

> I reckon he's still on the take

From behind, she noticed Twiggy slip his hand into his pocket and pull out his phone. He then gave an almost imperceptible nod.

'How much is Thornton paying you now?' Twiggy asked.

Dunbar paled. He clearly hadn't been expecting the question. 'Umm... nothing.'

'Try again. If you want immunity, then you better tell us everything.'

'Okay. I'm still on a retainer. But Thornton told me that the money was going to stop because he had to make economies. Whatever that meant.'

'I knew it,' Birdie said, glancing at Seb, who smiled his approval.

'Now the money has stopped, is this your way of getting your own back?' Twiggy asked.

'No. This is self-preservation. I have no intention of spending the rest of my life in prison for him.'

'I see. Moving on. Is Thornton capable of murder?' Sarge asked.

'Thornton?' Dunbar's eyes widened in genuine surprise. 'No way. He's the man behind the scenes. I doubt he's ever got dust on those expensive shoes of his, let alone blood.'

'We have evidence to suggest that he was responsible,' Sarge said, leaning forward slightly in his chair.

'So why do you need me?' Dunbar asked.

'Our evidence only takes us so far. We need your input.'

'I'm the icing on the cake,' Dunbar replied with a smirk.

'Don't get too cocky,' Twiggy snapped. 'You haven't got off yet.'

TWENTY-EIGHT

Thursday, 31 July

It was after four in the afternoon when Birdie's phone pinged with a text message. She snatched it from the pub table, where they'd been having a late lunch, her eyes bright.

'Thornton's finally at the station. Thank goodness. The delay's been killing me. He's refusing to speak without his solicitor present. Hardly surprising. Honestly, if you'd told me he'd left the country and joined North in Switzerland, I wouldn't have been surprised. Thank goodness he didn't.' Birdie got to her feet and scooped up her denim jacket. 'Let's go. The solicitor's due soon.'

Seb pushed back his chair and followed her across the pub, and they walked down the road to the station. They bumped into Twiggy as he emerged from Sergeant Weston's office. His mouth was strained and there were faint shadows under his eyes. It had been a long day for all of them, and it was far from over.

'Hey, Twig, has the solicitor arrived?' Birdie asked.

'Yes. A couple of minutes ago. We're almost ready for the interview. Be warned, Thornton isn't in a talkative mood. His solicitor's Roland White. Remember him from when you worked here?'

'Oh yes,' Birdie said with a grimace. 'He's certainly not known for representing good Samaritans. Then again, it's hardly surprising that Thornton has him on speed dial. Make sure not to let them fob you off.'

An offended look crossed Twiggy's face. 'Oh, suddenly you're the teacher, are you? Don't forget who let you sit in on your very first interview. I can assure you, Sarge and I will not be giving Thornton an easy ride. If we must give a slime bag like Dunbar immunity, you can be damn sure we're going to make it worthwhile.' Twiggy gave a solemn smile.

Twiggy stopped outside the door to wait for Sergeant Weston, while Birdie and Seb hurried to the observation area to take up their positions behind the one-way glass.

Thornton was sitting in the same seat that Dunbar had recently occupied. He wore a steel-grey suit and exuded a general air of indifference. Next to him, his solicitor, Roland White, leant over and whispered something in his ear.

The door to the interview room opened, and Sergeant Weston and Twiggy appeared. White immediately fixed them both with a hard glare.

'I demand to know what this is about. My client's a very busy man.'

Weston didn't respond as he settled into his chair and started the recording.

'Interview on the thirty-first of July, Those present: Detective Sergeant Weston, Detective Constable Branch, and—' He stopped and nodded across the table. 'Please state your names for the recording.'

'Roland White, solicitor.'

'William Jeremy Thornton.'

'Mr Thornton, you've been implicated in the murder of Helen Brackstone,' Sergeant Weston began, without any preamble.

'Murder?' Thornton slowly raised his left eyebrow and brushed a piece of non-existent dust from his expensive suit. 'Are you sure you have the right person?'

'One hundred per cent,' Sergeant Weston assured him. 'Would you care to tell us about it?'

'My client can hardly explain about something of which he has no knowledge,' White retorted with a roll of his eyes. He rose to his feet. 'Since it's clear this is a waste of our time, I suggest we end this farce.'

'Sit down, Mr White.' Sergeant Weston nodded at the chair. 'We have many more questions to ask. Mr Thornton, I repeat, what can you tell us about Helen Brackstone's murder?'

White opened his mouth, but Thornton put a restraining hand on his arm. 'It's okay, Roland.' He turned to face Weston and Twiggy. 'I have no idea who Helen Brackstone is.'

'She was poisoned in her house on the fifteenth of May, 1989. Are you sure you've never heard of her?' Twiggy checked.

'I am. Though it does sound like a tragedy,' Thornton said, his expression impassive.

'My client might not have heard of Helen Brackstone, but I have. I believe the murderer was apprehended, charged, and convicted. So why are we here?' White barked.

'New evidence has come to light that suggests your client was involved. This is his chance to cooperate. The CPS will look favourably on him if he does,' Sarge said with great restraint.

'No comment,' Thornton said, his mask not shifting.

Sergeant Weston extracted a piece of paper from the folder in front of him. 'This is an extract from the journal of a Colin

Howes. He refers to many jobs that you, Mr Thornton, hired him for. They include everything from intimidation through to working as a bodyguard. And – on the fifteenth of May, 1989 – accompanying you to Helen Brackstone's house. Let me read you what he wrote: "Thornton made me tie her up in a chair. I thought he was going to smack her around a bit. But then he pulled something out of his coat pocket and shoved it into her mouth. It was a bloody cyanide capsule." There's more, but I'm sure you get the gist.'

Sergeant Weston slid the piece of paper across the table, but Thornton didn't make any attempt to read it.

White leant forward and pushed the photocopied page away from them. 'A handwritten journal entry is hardly solid evidence. This is ridiculous.'

'Please instruct your client to answer,' Weston said.

'No comment.' Thornton gave him a stony glare.

'Interesting... We also have confirmation from a former police officer, Jeffrey Dunbar, that he was paid by you, Mr Thornton, to ensure Wes Brackstone was arrested for the murder and to pursue no other leads. You continued paying him over a period of years to provide information.'

'It sounds like you should concentrate on cleaning up your own house, if you're accusing one of your own of being corrupt,' White retorted.

'That's for us to worry about,' Sergeant Weston said. 'What do you have to say, Mr Thornton?'

'No comment,' Thornton said in a monotone, but a muscle in his jaw flickered.

Birdie spun around to face Seb. 'Hmm... Do you think he's figured out that Dunbar's done a deal with the police?'

'I'm sure he has,' Seb responded.

'We've also spoken to Joseph Pike,' Twiggy said. 'He was ordered by you to warn off Lucinda Bird, one of the private investigators who'd been hired to investigate the case. He did this by running her off the road and sending her a threatening text message. Each of these pieces of evidence might not stand up in court on their own, but together they form a strong case. What do you have to say?'

'No comment,' Thornton repeated and stared blankly ahead as Twiggy continued pushing him about Pike. But the replies were always the same.

No comment.

No comment.

No comment.

'I'll "no comment" him.' Birdie rolled her shoulders and stepped away from the glass, shaking off the energy that seemed to have filled her limbs. In the interview room, Twiggy's shoulders were tight, and it was clear he was becoming impatient. But Thornton continued staring impassively at the two police officers.

Seb's phone rang and he retrieved it from his pocket, putting it on speaker. 'It's Rob.'

'Hi, mate, how's the case going?' his friend asked.

'We're watching Thornton's interview. He's not cooperating but his solicitor's clearly perturbed.' Seb caught his friend up on what they'd discovered.

When he was finished, Rob let out a long whistle. 'You and Birdie have been busy.'

'You're telling me,' Birdie said. 'Hi, Rob, in case you didn't realise I was here, too.'

'Birdie, how are you?' Rob asked, sounding more cheerful than previously.

'I'll be better when we've nailed Thornton. What have you got for us?' Birdie asked.

'Hopefully, your winning hand,' Rob responded.

'You found phone calls between Thornton and North?' Birdie said, grinning in Seb's direction.

'Indeed I did. North called Thornton on the twenty-fourth of July at ten fifteen in the morning.'

'That's straight after we called him in Switzerland, and he hung up on us,' Seb said, his memory immediately allowing him to piece together the timeframe. 'I suspect that if we check Thornton's records, he would have called Joseph Pike not long after.'

'Who the hell's Pike?' Rob asked.

'He's the thug that Thornton hired to scare us off the case. He put a tracking device on Birdie's vehicle and ran her off the road.'

'What?' Rob asked. 'Are you okay, Birdie?'

'Of course I am. It takes more than a pathetic weasel like Pike to stop me. Thanks for the phone details – it ties everything up.'

'I have more to tell you,' Rob teased.

'What is it?' Birdie demanded, her eyes brimming with hope.

'Roger North tried to enter the country this morning and was arrested by the Met for tax evasion. That's why he was being investigated.'

'Why did he come back? He must have known the risk.' Seb drew his brows together.

North was a shrewd operator and he knew Seb and Birdie were investigating the old case. Was he back to deal with it personally? If so, he couldn't have realised that he was still a person of interest to the Met.

Either way, it was excellent news.

'No idea. Maybe he was getting squeezed by someone in Switzerland? I'm about to call the lead detective to update him on North's involvement with your cold case. I'm guessing the boys at Market Harborough will want to interview him at some stage.'

'I'm sure they will. Thanks for this,' Seb said.

'Yeah, thanks, Rob. See you soon,' Birdie added before Seb ended the call. 'You know what, if we tell Thornton that Dunbar's testifying against him and then he finds out that North's been arrested, it might encourage him to spill. What do you think?'

'I'll interrupt the interview and update them.'

TWENTY-NINE

Thursday, 31 July

Birdie followed Seb as he strode down the corridor and tapped on the door to the interview room. There was a shuffling noise, and several moments later, Sarge and Twiggy both appeared, closing the door behind them. Their faces were etched with frustration from so far getting nowhere.

'This better be because you have something for us?' Sarge said. 'I don't want to ease up on this little shit.'

'Is he getting to you?' Birdie asked, noting the tight set of Sarge's jaw.

'What do you think?' Sarge responded, his fists clenched. 'But I can sit there all day and listen to his *no comment* if that's what it takes, even if he does think he's playing us.'

'Well, you won't need to,' Birdie said, barely containing her excitement. 'Tell him, Seb.'

Her partner squared his shoulders. 'An ex-colleague from the Met informed me that Roger North contacted Thornton immediately after we'd phoned him. Also, North arrived in the country this morning and was arrested for tax evasion. You could imply to Thornton that North is going to assist in the Met's enquiries. It might encourage him to admit to his role in the murder.'

Sarge let out a gruff bark of laughter that echoed down the corridor. 'Thanks, Clifford. This is good.' He nodded at Twiggy, a predatory smile spreading across his face. 'Now, let's see what our guest has to say.'

Once Sarge and Twiggy had disappeared into the interview room, Birdie and Seb returned to their positions in the observation area. Through the one-way glass, the fluorescent lights cast harsh shadows across the face of their suspect.

'Look at the solicitor.' Birdie practically cackled with glee, pressing closer to the glass. 'He's clearly stressed to the eyeballs. Watch how he keeps adjusting his tie.'

Sarge and Twiggy sat down to continue the interview, but there was a noticeable shift in the room's energy, like the air before a thunderstorm. Thornton was as still as a statue, his expensive suit no longer projecting authority but instead hanging on him like armour with too many chinks. White's face was pale with his arms folded. Sweat beaded at his hairline. It was as if they'd already guessed their time was up.

'We have an update on your friend Roger North,' Sarge said, appearing deceptively casual.

'How's that relevant?' White asked, his voice cracking slightly.

Thornton's impenetrable mask slipped and his fingers fluttered against the table like trapped birds.

'Ha.' Birdie let out a satisfied shout, elbowing Seb in triumph.

'You might like to ask your client,' Twiggy said, leaning forward slightly.

'He was arrested this morning while returning to England,' Sarge said, before White had the chance to reply. Each word landing like a hammer blow.

'For what?' Thornton demanded, his composure finally breaking.

'We're not at liberty to say,' Sarge continued, drawing out the moment. 'But we've been given to understand that he's going to be most cooperative, if you get what I mean.'

'You go, Sarge,' Birdie whispered, pressing her palms against the glass.

'In light of this information, do you now wish to comment on the case?' Sarge's voice hardened. 'I'd take this opportunity if I were you,' he added, sitting back in his chair.

The room fell silent as Thornton rubbed his chin, his eyes dark and calculating. The clock on the wall ticked loudly, marking each second of his crumbling resolve.

Finally, he looked directly at Sarge, desperation in his gaze. 'If I tell you everything you must note that I'm cooperating fully.'

'What the hell?' Thornton's solicitor muttered, slumping back in his chair.

'Duly noted,' Sarge responded. 'Now, did you kill Helen Brackstone?' Sarge's words cut through the tension like a knife.

'Yes,' Thornton growled, as if a knife was pushed against the artery in his neck. His façade of control was completely shattered as the words spilled out. 'I killed the woman, but it was Roger North who gave the instruction.'

THIRTY

Thursday, 31 July

After a quick celebratory drink in the pub close to the police station, Birdie and Seb drove towards Northampton Road, to visit Daryl so they could give her the good news.

The traffic was light, and it wasn't long before they were pulling up outside their client's home. Daryl had returned from Dorset the previous day, after it had been agreed that the danger was now passed. As she opened the door, a smile broke out on her face.

'You have news, don't you?'

'Is it that obvious?' Birdie said, pleased Daryl had some colour back in her cheeks.

'Detectives aren't the only ones who can read people. Teachers can, too. Come in. We'll sit in the conservatory – it's lovely at this time of year.' Daryl turned and led them to the rear of the house.

Nestled in the bright room was a gracefully curved wicker sofa, with crisp white and green floral cushions, flanked by two matching armchairs.

'This is lovely,' Birdie said, dropping down onto one of the easy chairs.

Daryl sat on the other and Seb chose the middle of the sofa, stretching his legs out in front of him.

'Thanks. They're new.' Daryl drew in a breath. 'Okay... tell me everything.'

'We've discovered who murdered your mother, and it wasn't your father,' Birdie said gently.

'Oh.' A tiny gasp escaped Daryl's lips as a range of emotions flashed across her face. 'I'm... I'm not sure what to say. After all this time... Are you sure?' Daryl glanced from Birdie to Seb.

'Yes,' Seb said. 'We can't give many details, other than the police have officially re-opened the case and we expect your father to be exonerated. It's a long process and you may wish to consult a solicitor.'

Daryl buried her face in her hands and let out a muffled sob. All those wasted years she'd been without a father, her own daughter without a grandfather... How different things might have been? Instead, Wes had died in jail, never knowing who was to blame.

They were silent for a long time before Daryl finally looked up. Tears glistened on her dark lashes and she wiped them away with a tissue.

'Thank you both. I know this won't bring my parents back, but it does mean I can have a proper memorial service. I'd be honoured if you would both attend.'

'We will,' Seb assured her.

'I'm going to invite Ali Simmons as well. If she hadn't decided to investigate the case for her podcast, I might never have contacted you. If you'll excuse me, I want to call my daughter to let her know.'

Birdie got to her feet, closely followed by Seb. 'We'll leave you to talk privately. The police will be in touch at some time, and, I'm afraid, so will the media.'

'Now we know the truth, I'm prepared for anything.' Daryl followed them to the front door. Despite the shock in her eyes, her whole posture had changed. It was as if years of worry had vanished. Birdie wasn't sure she'd ever get sick of being able to make a difference in someone's life.

THIRTY-ONE

Sunday, 3 August

'That was Ali. I've got to admit, I'm impressed,' Birdie said, as Seb came back from the bar and placed a glass of cider in front of her on the table.

'About what?' he said, sitting opposite her.

Birdie picked up her glass and took a sip. 'The series starts airing next week, a little earlier than she'd originally planned, and she's already recorded an interview with Daryl. This means she'll be ahead of everyone else once the case becomes public knowledge. Oh, and while you were at the bar, I told her you'd be happy to recreate the moment you discovered the tracking device on my car.'

'Did you indeed?' Seb studied his business partner, who had a deadpan expression on her face.

He was almost certain Birdie was joking, and although he agreed that the podcaster approached her work with integrity, he still wasn't sure how he felt about the crossover between serious investigations and the realm of content creation.

'Not really... but your face was a picture when I said it.'

Birdie smirked. 'Joking aside, Ali said thanks for sending through the case details and she asked if she could interview us. I told her we'd discuss it and get back to her. You know it would be great publicity.'

'For what?' He raised an eyebrow. 'I don't believe being connected to a podcast will enhance our reputation.'

'Nonsense. No publicity is bad publicity. It will be a great way to bring in more business,' Birdie said, sounding excited.

'We already have a healthy workload, and next week, we have discussions with a potential client regarding insurance fraud,' he reminded her.

'Insurance fraud is so boring... Although maybe not so bad as cheating spouses. But there's room for us to expand. We helped bring down Thornton and North – that's going to keep our names out there, alongside the other high-profile cases we've done. Go on, Seb... Think about it, please... I've seen a gorgeous little terraced house close to the river, and a couple more big cases could tip the balance and the bank will give me a good mortgage offer.'

'It doesn't actually work like that,' Seb said, taking a sip of his beer.

'I said it for effect.' Birdie waved a dismissive hand. 'But I'm still up for putting ourselves out there.'

'Have you made an offer on the property?'

'I'm close, but before I do, will you come and view it? I want to make sure my abnormally tall friends can get through the doorway.'

'I'm sure it will be fine – I instinctively duck wherever I go.'

'I hadn't noticed, but now you mention it... So, is that a yes?'

'It is. Your parents will miss you when you've gone.'

'You'd think so, but thanks to my two brothers being at home for the summer holidays, I'm sure Mum's longing for the day she becomes an empty nester. Besides, I'll be thirty in a few months. I'm way past wanting to share a bathroom... unless it's with someone special.'

A soft flush rose up her neck, and Seb blinked. That was new.

'Is there something else you want to tell me?'

An almost shy smile tugged at her mouth. 'I went on a date last night. It was pretty cool.'

'Oh, I see.'

Seb studied Birdie. Despite her head-on approach to work, when it came to her personal life, she was reserved and kept things close to her chest.

Was he meant to ask for details?

The uncertainty must have been clear on his face because Birdie burst out laughing, sounding back to her usual self.

'Melinda's the cousin of one of my cricket teammates. She's a librarian and moved here recently for a new job. Okay?'

'A librarian?' Seb's mouth dropped open as he tried to recall the last time he'd seen Birdie read a novel. Or sit still for more than ten minutes. His mouth twitched, but she shot him a warning glance.

'Whatever you're thinking, stop it. Opposites can attract. Anyway, it's early days, but so far... so good. You know, I'd forgotten how nice it is to meet someone who really gets you. Plus, getting dressed up and leaving the house is fun. You should try it sometime.' She waved her empty glass. 'It's my shout. Unless you have something pressing to do on a Sunday afternoon, like... Umm, I don't know... checking the accounts?'

'I'm sure I can fit in another drink.' He repressed a smile and passed over his glass.

As Birdie disappeared inside towards the bar, Seb leant against his chair and let the atmosphere wash over him. The ebb and flow of conversation around him was punctuated by the clink of glasses and the off-key strum of a guitar being tuned up by the one of the members of a small folk band in the corner.

Seb was pleased that Birdie was considering putting in an offer on her first home and was on the precipice of a new relationship. She worked hard and excelled at whatever she put her mind to. Having gone through some difficult years while searching for her birth mother, she deserved to be happy.

Although her quip implying that he needed to get a life had stung a little. Especially since he was in no hurry to change the status quo. He was perfectly happy with how things were progressing. Perhaps he should remind her that he was not only older than she was, but he was also on his second career and had had his fair share of relationships.

Hence why he was enjoying the slower pace of life and was in no hurry to change it. Even if Birdie believed he was an old stick in the mud...

'Penny for them.' Birdie's voice dragged him back to reality as she placed a pint of beer in front of him and studied his expression. 'You were miles away. Dreaming of anything exciting?'

'Yes. A nice, relaxed meal tonight with my daughter and dog for company. Speaking of which, she should be here soon. I thought she'd like to join our celebration, since she worked on the case.'

'She's already here. I saw her at the bar and tried to buy her a drink, but she said she'd get it herself. How weird is that? Who says no to a free drink?'

'Yesterday you were admiring how independent she was,' Seb reminded her as a familiar figure appeared at the sliding doors separating the courtyard from the rest of the pub.

Keira scanned the area until her eyes landed on them. Her wide mouth broke into a smile, and she threaded her way past the many tables towards them. She was tanned from the summer and her cheeks were glowing as she clutched a bottle of beer.

'Oh, buying the fancy stuff, are you?' Birdie quipped.

Keira wrinkled her nose. 'I like the taste of it. Sorry I'm late... we got held up.'

'That's fine,' Seb said, lifting his glass to take a sip of his drink before suddenly frowning.

Wait. Did she say we?

As if on cue, Keira swivelled around and smiled at someone behind her. A guy who looked to be in his early twenties stepped forward. He was the same height as Keira and had an almost identical tan, with sun-bleached hair and green eyes.

'Dad. Birdie. This is Hamish.' Keira tucked an arm into his and dragged him forward.

Hamish gave Birdie a lopsided smile, and then swallowed and turned to look directly at Seb.

'Nice to meet you, my lord.'

'What?' Birdie snorted. 'Did you tell him to say that?'

Seb hardly noticed as his attention went back to his daughter, who was entirely focused on Hamish. Suddenly it seemed like he'd missed a vital part of the conversation.

The one where his daughter had a boyfriend.

Seb's head was all over the place. How on earth was he to deal with this revelation?

'Don't call him that. He's Seb, or Dad – well, to me – but not "my lord". Plus that's not even how you address the son of a viscount.'

'Okay,' Hamish said with a shrug. Not seeming at all bothered by his error.

'Even if it was right, we don't do that sort of stuff. We're normal people,' Keira said with a smile. 'Now, let's sit down. My feet are killing me. We went hiking this morning. It was so gorgeous. Hamish is into climbing and has been showing me the ropes. Anyway, now we've arrived, the celebrations can begin. Here's to closing the case.'

Seb continued staring at the young man, a wave of irritation rising through him. He went to open his mouth, but before any words could come out, Birdie shot him a warning look and patted the chair next to her.

'Hamish, come and sit here. It's nice to meet you.'

'You, too. K's told me all about you both.' Hamish settled into the chair and put down his untouched beer while Keira dragged another chair over, so she was sitting between Hamish and Seb.

Seb's skin prickled. *K?* Since when did Keira have a nickname?

Seb opened his mouth to speak again, only this time when Birdie shot him a sharp glance, he ignored it. 'Has she indeed? Because we know nothing about you.'

'Dad,' Keira groaned. 'Please don't go all weird on me. You've been busy, so I didn't want to distract you.'

'Well, you have my full attention now,' he assured her. He turned to face Hamish. 'Tell me about yourself and where you met my daughter.'

'I'm studying law at Lenchester,' Hamish replied, staring directly at Seb. 'But I grew up in Cambridge. Keira and I met at a party.'

'Hamish found Cambridge too snooty and wanted to move away.' Keira beamed at Seb. 'Isn't that cool?'

'Lenchester?' Seb's jaw tightened. 'Is that why you want to transfer? Because of a boy?'

'Boy? Hamish is twenty-one.' Keira stared at him, her dark eyes wide. 'Didn't you and Mum meet at uni?'

'That's hardly relevant,' Seb said.

Before he could say anything else, Birdie shifted in her chair to properly face Hamish. 'Law? How are you finding it? One of my brothers has just finished his first year at Durham and he said it sucked his brain dry.'

Hamish let out a reluctant laugh. 'I hear you. It's intense, but I'm enjoying it. I'm particularly interested in studying international human rights law.'

'He's super smart.' Keira beamed with pride.

Hamish shook his head. 'You're the smart one.'

'You're just saying that because I chose you,' Keira teased.

'No way. It's because you don't rely solely on your HSAM to get through your work. You do proper research and work hard to apply it.'

Keira's cheeks reddened at the compliment.

Seb folded his arms, unable to quell the turmoil growing inside of him. Birdie caught his eye and gave a tiny shake of her head.

What?

Was she trying to tell him to relax? Easy for her to say – Keira wasn't her daughter.

But one thing he was sure of, after being apart from Keira for most of her young life, he wasn't prepared to alienate her now, and as the Sunday afternoon stretched on, Seb found his initial tension slowly melting away.

He watched Keira, her face alight with laughter, as she regaled them with her climbing mishaps, and how Hamish looked on, his affection apparent.

Seb realised at that moment that life was very much like the cases they solved: full of unexpected twists and sometimes those twists – even those involving surprise boyfriends – were acceptable.

A LETTER FROM THE AUTHOR

Dear reader,

Huge thanks for reading *Question of Guilt*. I hope you are hooked on the Detective Sebastian Clifford series. If you want to join other readers in hearing all about my new books, you can sign up here:

> www.stormpublishing.co/sally-rigby

If you enjoyed this book and could spare a few moments to leave a review that would be hugely appreciated. Even a short review can make all the difference in encouraging a reader to discover my books for the first time. Thank you so much!

Thanks again for being part of this amazing journey with me and I hope you'll stay in touch – I have so many more stories and ideas to entertain you with!

Sally Rigby

facebook.com/Sally-Rigby-131414630527848
instagram.com/sally.rigby.author

ACKNOWLEDGEMENTS

Writing a book is never a solitary endeavour, and this one would not have been possible without the support of so many wonderful people.

First and foremost, I must thank my friend Amanda Ashby, who has been there from the very beginning. Her unwavering support and brilliant insights have made this journey not just possible, but enjoyable. Thank you for being my sounding board and cheerleader rolled into one.

To my incredible editors at Storm Publishing – Claire Boyd and Rebecca Millar – your expertise and dedication have shaped this book into something I'm truly proud of. Claire, it's been a total pleasure working with you. Rebecca, your enthusiasm for this project and thoughtful suggestions have been invaluable.

The entire team at Storm Publishing deserves recognition for their tireless work behind the scenes. From Oliver Rhodes and Kathryn Taussig to the editorial staff who polished every word, the production team who brought everything together, and the creative minds in cover design who captured the essence of the story perfectly – thank you all.

I'd also like to mention Daryl Brackstone, who won a charity contest to have a character named after her. Thanks for entering. I hope you enjoy seeing your name in print.

Finally, to my family, who have put up with my endless hours at the computer, late meals, and distant looks when plotting scenes in my head – your patience and understanding mean the world to me.

Printed in Great Britain
by Amazon